LOSING LEO

A Strong Man's Hand - Book Six

KAT CARRINGTON

Published by Blushing Books
An Imprint of
ABCD Graphics and Design, Inc.
A Virginia Corporation
977 Seminole Trail #233
Charlottesville, VA 22901

Kat Carrington
Losing Leo

Print ISBN: 978-1-63954-143-0
v1

Cover Art by ABCD Graphics & Design

Chapter 1

Shelby hugged her grandmother and said, "Good morning, Gran! I know I'm early, but I just couldn't wait to get started. I hope you don't mind."

GG Beauchamp chuckled and said, "Of course not. Would you like a cup of tea? And how is our little one this morning?"

Shelby made a face. "Determined to crush my bladder, I think. I'm so glad it's almost time for him to make his appearance. I never dreamed I'd make so many trips to the bathroom when I should be sleeping peacefully."

GG laughed. "It's to prepare you for all the times you'll have to be getting up *after* he *or she* gets here."

"Oh, I didn't think about that."

"Just make up your mind that you need to sleep whenever your baby does and let Sam worry about everything else. At least for a while." GG poured two cups of tea and stirred some honey into them both.

"I just want you to know, Gran, how much it means to me that you're telling me the whole story of you and Grandpa.

You two had such a beautiful love story and I can't wait to share it."

GG smiled and said, "Your grandpa was a very special man."

"I know he was and I bet he'd say the same thing about you."

GG's smile turned a little mischievous. "He really did spoil me to death most of the time. He did make me toe the line now and then, though."

Shelby's cheeks were a little pink. "How was it that you put it?"

GG said with a wink, "A strong man's hand can be a very good thing."

Shelby had to giggle. "Well, I'm ready to begin whenever you are."

"Let's do it." They settled comfortably in front of the fireplace and Shelby turned on her recorder and opened her notebook.

The tall man, still lean and fit, even with the gray scattered through his dark hair, leaned his forehead against the tree trunk and counted out loud, loudly enough to be heard across the large yard. There was the sound of an excited giggle and the big Golden Retriever raced in circles at the edge of the yard by a cluster of bushes, barking excitedly as he romped.

A voice called, trying to be quiet, "Rowdy! Go away! Go find Shelby!"

The dog raced across the yard and the man reached the number one hundred and then called loudly, "Ready or not, here I come!"

A small figure darted across the yard as he turned and started away from her, then froze as he turned and spotted her.

Stopping as if he were confused, he looked in both directions and then took a few steps toward her. Another small figure crept out of the shadows of the garden shed and advanced toward the big tree until the dog ran to her, jumping up and down in his excitement. The man turned to see where the dog was going and changed directions again, starting toward the child and dog and leaving the other little girl convulsed with giggles. They were quite sure they were tricking him into chasing one of them, then the other until suddenly he turned and they both reached the big tree, just escaping his clutches. They hugged each other, jumping up and down and laughing hysterically.

"We did it! We did it!"

They both let out screams as he ran up behind them and snatched them up, holding one of them under each arm and jogging around the yard in triumph. GG Beauchamp had come out the back door during their game and was sitting on the deck laughing at them all. Her husband, Leo, carried the girls over to her, grinning and bending over to kiss her as he set the two little girls down.

"Gran, did you see?" one of the dark-haired four-year-olds asked.

"We beat Paw-Paw to the tree!" her identical twin sister said in triumph.

"I did see. You were so fast!"

Leo held his hands up in surrender. "I have to admit, you won fair and square."

"Rowdy always finds us and he tells on us," the first little girl said.

GG chuckled. "Yes, it's pretty hard to hide when Rowdy's around. Who wants a cookie?"

Before the girls could answer, Leo said, "Me! Me!" It made his granddaughters giggle again and GG passed cookies out to them all.

The two little girls were truly identical, with shoulder length, shiny dark hair and brilliant sapphire blue eyes. But Shelby was quieter and gentler than her more temperamental sister, Savannah, although both of them were soft hearted and loving. Leo doted on them both and GG adored them; she could never get enough of them and if she could have changed one thing in her life, it would be to magically make her son and daughter-in-law love the tiny town of Boone, Indiana, just as much as she and Leo did. But they loved living in the city and they had ever since they'd met in college. She had long ago accepted the fact that they were never going to live in Boone. She was just grateful that the girls loved spending time there and their parents were generous with their visits.

"Paw-Paw, can we go see the horses tomorrow?" Savannah asked, turning her big blue eyes on her grandfather.

"Horses? What horses? We don't have any horses." Leo loved teasing them.

"Paw-Paw! You know, the horses we always go see! Miss Mamie's horses!" Savannah's tone was outraged.

"Hmm. I'll have to think about that. Horses might make me sneeze."

Savannah laughed hysterically at the idea of her grandfather reduced to sneezing around horses. He winked at her and she beamed at him, knowing she would get to see her beloved horses the next day.

Shelby said, "I wish Carter was here. He likes the horses too."

Leo nodded wisely and said, "I know he does, but his Cub Scout camping trip is very important to him."

"I don't think I'd like to sleep in a tent. What if a bear came around?" Shelby looked worried.

Savannah said, "There aren't any bears in Indiana, silly."

She thought for a moment and then said, "There aren't, are there, Paw-Paw?"

"No, so far Indiana doesn't have any bears," Leo said with a wink.

"Well, girls, who wants to help me make dinner?" GG asked.

"I do!" said Shelby, scrambling to her feet. "Can we make biscuits again?"

"We can make biscuits anytime," GG promised.

Savannah said, "I'm going to help Paw-Paw take Rowdy for a walk."

"Okay," said GG. "Make sure Paw-Paw doesn't start sneezing around Rowdy."

Both girls giggled and GG winked at Savannah. Shelby and GG made Swiss steak and mashed potatoes with green beans and a basket full of biscuits with GG's homemade strawberry jam. After dinner, the girls had their bath with mountains of bubbles and then they all played Candyland together until GG could see the signs of bedtime coming on and she turned on a children's movie they could all watch together. Half an hour later, her little granddaughters were sound asleep on the couch, snuggled against their sleeping grandfather and GG laughed quietly to herself.

She whispered into his ear, "Leo, let's get these babies to bed."

He blinked slowly awake and looked down at the peacefully sleeping little girls and sent up a little prayer of thanks for the richness of his life. He carried the girls up to the room they had fixed up for them, the room that had once been his sisters, Molly and Ginny's room. Their house had held Beauchamps for several generations and when his parents had been ready to retire to Florida, he and GG and James had moved into it. Filling it with family, especially grandchildren, had always been GG's dream. They tucked the little girls in, turned on the nightlight and went down the hall to their own room.

"I locked up downstairs and I brought us up a glass of wine," GG said softly.

"Good." Leo kissed her and said, "We'll just watch a little TV in bed; that way we'll be close to them."

GG went into the bathroom and changed into her pajamas and when she came out, it was Leo's turn. She put her arms around him and lifted her face for his kiss. He gave a little growl and said, "Are you trying to tempt me, gorgeous?"

She shook her head and gave a little laugh. "You're so silly. I'm not gorgeous. I'm getting old. I'm getting gray hair and wrinkles, and even though I try to stay in shape, everything is starting to sag."

Her husband put a finger under her chin and looked directly into her eyes. "Don't ever say that again. You're a beautiful woman, GG, more beautiful now than when you were a girl because of the life you've lived, the courage you've shown, the love and compassion you've given. When I look at you, I see all of it, the girl, the woman, the love. I especially see the love that shines from you every minute of every day. How could you be anything but beautiful? Gray hair means nothing, wrinkles aren't ugly, they're a mark of character. Your body bore my son; how could the effects that had on you be ugly to me? So don't ever doubt me when I call you gorgeous."

GG's eyes were shimmering with tears at the words he said to her. "Oh, Leo, how was I ever lucky enough to find you?"

His eyes gleamed. "I was the lucky one. I was lucky that you were so stubborn and determined to get your own way when you were a girl that I had to rescue you from the mob at that Vietnam protest. And that was the beginning of our love story; you thought I was an arrogant, bossy asshole and hoped you'd never see me again."

GG was laughing softly. "And I was so shocked when I

found out that you were living right here in Boone! And luckily, it turned out that I was wrong and you were even more stubborn than me."

He shot her a look of innocence. "I was stubborn?"

"Yep, you wouldn't give up on me and you made me fall in love with you."

"I had to. You would have gotten yourself into all kinds of trouble if I hadn't been there to get you out of it."

"Don't forget, Sharon and I managed to go to a music festival for a whole weekend and nobody ever even found out. And we didn't get into a bit of trouble." GG looked quite proud of herself.

"I'd never forget that. You were a rebel." He kissed her on the tip of her nose, remembering her in her faded bellbottomed jeans with her beads and her long, straight hair falling below her shoulders, with one tiny braid swinging alongside her face, a feather braided into it. She had taken his breath away, and the knowledge of how young she was, scared him to death. He had been twenty-two and she was only seventeen, but he couldn't get her out of his mind and he had ended up waiting for her until she turned eighteen and graduated from high school. They'd been married a few months after graduation and their lives since then had been a rough journey at times, but one that they always traveled together.

They clinked their glasses together and toasted each other, smiling softly as they looked back at their memories. They had their heartaches to look back on, some that had been almost more than they could bear, but they had managed to come through them together and, in the end, they'd been stronger for it. And when they looked back at it all, the joys outweighed the sorrows by far. Leo still enjoyed his full-time engineering position and GG still ran the arts and crafts gift shop that Leo had bought for her when their son, James, went off to college. The shop, GG's Gems, had become a part of the little town of

Boone; it showcased the work of local artists and craftsmen and women and people came from all around to shop there.

James was their only child, but he and his wife, Allison, had three children, Carter, who was seven and the twins, three years younger than their big brother. So Leo and GG had their family, perhaps not as big a family as they had once envisioned, but enough to fill the house with noise and laughter when they were all there. Both GG's parents and Leo's had lived to see their great-grandchildren; Leo's father had passed away a couple of years ago and his mother had chosen to stay in their Florida community where she had lots of friends and one of Leo's sisters, Molly, nearby. GG's parents had retired and bought themselves a motorhome that they lived in, determined to visit every state before they would sell it and pick one spot to live in. They had friends everywhere they went; they were still healthy and when the family gathered at Leo and GG's home, they loved to come and join them whenever they were able to.

GG's brother, Carl, had finished his master's degree before he married his wife and settled down to raise a family. Quite the opposite, his twin, Bryce, had made a name for himself as an investigative journalist and had never married after he'd had a short, tragic marriage in name only with a Vietnamese girl he'd met on assignment. He'd received numerous awards for excellence in journalism and they got to see him often on TV. He visited home when he could and it was usually a complete surprise to the family when he would pop in. He had his choice of assignments and he went to the most dangerous places in the world often. He had a thirst for adventure and a strong need to share the true events of the world with the public.

Savannah was awake first, as usual. She peeked in the door at her grandparents and crept over to Leo's side of the bed.

"Paw-Paw," she said in a loud whisper, "it's daytime out."

When he didn't stir, she reached over and touched his eyelid, light as a feather, and stroked upward to open his eye.

The touch startled Leo, but he realized immediately what it was and struggled to keep from laughing. She was reaching over to touch the other eye when he jumped and whispered, "What are you doing?"

Savannah squealed and jerked her hand back as she jumped about a foot in the air, she was so startled. Leo laughed and reached out to pull her up onto the bed.

"Well, good morning, Shelby."

She forgot to be quiet, exclaiming, "I'm not Shelby!"

Leo squinted at her, looking her over for several seconds and finally said, "Oh, I guess you're not."

"Paw-Paw, you know I'm always the first one up."

GG groaned, "Yes, she is. Is the sun even up?"

Savannah said, "It's been up *forever!*"

Leo chuckled. "I'll tell you what; you go down and let Rowdy out in the back yard and we'll get up."

"Okay!" She scrambled off the bed.

Leo called, "Walk! And be careful on the steps."

Savannah slowed down and he could see her grip the handrail carefully as she started down the stairs. Leo leaned over and kissed GG. "Give me five minutes in the bathroom, then take your time getting up. I'll see if Shelby's awake."

A few minutes later, GG could hear him talking to Shelby and then she saw the two of them heading down the stairs together. She lay back for just a second and then sighed and got out of bed, stretching as she went. When she started down the stairs herself, she could smell the coffee Leo had started and she thanked him silently. There was plenty of chatter coming from the kitchen and GG went straight toward the coffeepot, where her husband handed her a steaming cup, already prepared the way she liked it.

"God bless you," she said fervently, cautiously taking the first sip and then sighing in bliss.

"You used to be much more of a morning person," Leo observed.

"Yeah, I was younger then."

He laughed at her and gave her a kiss.

"Don't worry; coffee will fix it," she said, taking another sip.

It was a good thing she had her coffee early. The phone rang about twenty minutes later and it was James. After she hung up, she said, "Carter fell out of a tree and hurt his arm. James and Allison are headed to the emergency room, the scout leader is taking him straight there. They think it's probably broken."

"Is he all right?" Shelby asked anxiously.

"Oh, yes, it hurts some but he'll be fine. You daddy did almost exactly the same thing when he was Carter's age."

Her eyes were huge. "He *did?"*

"He sure did. And he was just fine."

Savannah shook her head solemnly. "He should have come with us," she said wisely.

GG and Leo had to laugh. Leo looked at his wife inquiringly and she nodded. "He'll be fine. Now, let's keep busy until they call us again. What should we have for breakfast today?"

Savannah crowed, "French toast!"

Shelby said, "Yeah, with strawberries."

"And bacon," Leo chimed in.

"All right, strawberry French toast and bacon it is." GG began to bustle around the kitchen and Savannah went to let Rowdy in.

"Paw-Paw, can I feed Rowdy?" asked Savannah.

"I'm sure Rowdy would like that." He watched Savannah go to the pantry with Rowdy's bowl and struggle to open the lid of the big plastic bin that held his dog food. He knew better than to offer to help her and, after a couple of tries, she got it open. She measured out the right amount of food and closed the lid before she brought the bowl back with Rowdy dancing around her, eager for his breakfast.

Shelby went to the front porch and got the Sunday paper, bringing it in to Leo. After breakfast, he would sit with both girls in his lap and read the comic pages to them. Then he would be left in peace long enough to get part of the paper read, starting with the sports section. When the girls weren't there, he liked to watch the Sunday morning news shows, but he didn't attempt that when they were keeping the grandkids. By the time he got the paper read, GG would have the girls dressed, teeth brushed, and hair up in ponytails, ready for their visit to go see Miss Mamie's horses. It was the perfect way to spend a spring Sunday morning in Boone, Indiana.

Chapter 2

James called later in the day and let GG know that Carter had, indeed, broken his left arm and was in a cast. He was tired and sore, but most of all he was mad because he'd had to miss the rest of the day with his Cub Scout troop.

GG laughed. "That sounds like Carter. You were mad because you got knocked out of the football game."

James said, "Well, yeah, I had to miss the rest of the whole season."

His mother pointed out, "Well, you *were* only nine. You had plenty of football in your life after that."

"I did get all the kids to make a fuss over my cast. Anyway, we'd like to know if you'd be able to keep the girls for another night. We'd really like to get him home and resting. But I know you both have work tomorrow, so if it's any problem at all, I'll take Allison and Carter home and then I'll come and get them."

"Don't be silly. Go home and spoil your boy for the rest of the day. We'll be fine tomorrow. Monday's a slow day for my shop and I close fairly often on Mondays. I never schedule any artist meetings on Mondays, so it won't be a problem at all. And you know your dad; he's more or less the boss at his firm now. He never has a problem taking a day off when he wants one." GG didn't mind a bit getting an extra day with the girls.

"Are they there? I can tell them how their brother is doing."

GG said, "No, Leo took them over to see the horses. But we can call you when they get back here."

James said, "I'm not sure exactly when we'll get home, so I'll call you. We'd just like to talk to them, tell them about Carter, and tell them we miss them."

GG felt the warm glow of love wash over her. Even if they only had the kids for a day, James and Allison often called to talk to them. It pleased GG enormously when she reflected on what good parents they had turned out to be. James held the phone so she could say hello to Carter and commiserate with him over his injury for a minute and then they had to go. When Leo and the girls came back, they were bubbling over with talk about the horses.

Shelby said, "I wish you came, Gran."

"I know, sweetie, but I needed to stay here in case your mom and dad called. And they did and guess what? You get to stay an extra day!"

The girls both cheered, but then Shelby looked worried. "What about Carter? Is he okay?"

"He is. I even got to talk to him for a minute. He broke his left arm and it's in a cast, like the one that his friend, Tyler, had in the wintertime, remember? He's just tired and sore and your dad wanted to take him home so he could get some rest instead of driving all the way here."

Savannah said, "Carter doesn't drive. All he does is sit in the back and bug Daddy about how long it's going to take to get there."

GG and Leo laughed and Leo said, "But taking a long ride right after you break your arm is not exactly fun."

Savannah considered that and said, "I guess. And, besides, Mom's going to want to go home and fuss over him. I think it makes her feel better."

Shelby said, "I'm going to fuss over him too."

Her sister said, "You go ahead. He's going to make you do *everything* for him, wait and see."

GG's shoulders were shaking with laughter and Leo looked at her gravely. "She's right; he will do exactly that."

Savannah tilted her head and asked, "Was he really okay, Gran?"

"Yes, he was mad because he had to miss the rest of the day camping."

"Okay, then I'm not gonna fuss over him." Savannah ran off to play with Rowdy.

Shelby said, "I'll help Mommy fuss over him. I don't even care if he makes me do stuff for him."

GG patted her on the head. "That's my girl. You like to take care of people, don't you?"

Shelby nodded vigorously. "Yep. I'm gonna be a doctor when I grow up. The kind that takes care of dogs and horses."

Leo said softly, "James better get that promotion he's going after." He and GG both laughed.

The girls were happy to talk to their brother later and took turns talking to both their parents, and it was obvious that Carter was going to milk his injury for all it was worth. Finally, James got back on the phone with Leo. "He's getting a little too much fun out of this, I think."

Leo laughed and said, "Takes after his dad."

James chuckled and said, "You have to let people fuss over you when the opportunity presents itself. But, seriously, I think he's really starting to hurt now. They gave us something for him to take to help with pain and let him sleep so after he eats,

I think it'll be time for that. I'll call you before we head your way tomorrow."

"Okay, James, we'll see you tomorrow."

Savannah said, "Gran, we're hungry."

GG said, "Well, it's lunchtime, so that makes sense. I'll make lunch now." She made the girls their favorite peanut butter and jelly sandwiches along with bowls of chicken noodle soup and fixed Leo a sandwich of leftover Swiss steak, while she settled for a salad.

Leo mowed the yard while the girls napped, worn out after the excitement of visiting the horses. Some days they napped and other days they didn't; in one more year, they would be in kindergarten and too grown up for naps. Sometimes it was shocking to GG when she realized how fast they were growing up. She wished she could keep them little for longer and she knew Allison felt the same way. Today turned out to be a real nap day and the two little girls were asleep for nearly two hours. When they got up, they had a cookie and finished their milk from lunch before they went outside to join Leo and Rowdy. GG went out to watch them; Leo had bought a flat of begonias to plant along each side of the garden shed and both girls were eager to help. So they dug in the dirt and Leo showed them how to put the little plants in and tuck them into the soil. They handled the little plants gently and when they were finished with the first side, the row of flowers was a little crooked but they had done a good job.

"Hi, GG!" came a call and Katie came through the gate from the side of the house.

"Katie! Come on back here!" GG hurried to meet her friend and they exchanged heartfelt hugs. They'd been close friends since high school, along with their other third, Sharon, and they considered themselves sisters.

Leo waved at them and the girls called out their hellos.

"I brought a bottle of wine," Katie said, holding out the chilled bottle of white wine.

"Sounds good. Are we celebrating?" GG asked.

"We are. Let's pour the wine and then I'll tell you."

They went together to the kitchen and GG poured the wine and put the bottle in an ice bucket before they carried their glasses back out to the deck and settled into chairs under the umbrella.

"Look at them; they're so cute," Katie said, watching the girls.

"You mean the girls, not Leo, right?" GG teased.

"I don't know, he's still pretty cute too," Katie said with a laugh. "But, yes, I was talking about them. They just love to do things with him, don't they?"

"Yes, especially Savannah. Carter broke his arm this morning falling out of a tree at his Cub Scout camp out."

Her friend gasped. "Oh, no! Is he okay?"

"Yes, he's fine. I'm sure it hurts, but he's going to seriously enjoy all the attention he's about to get."

"Boys!" Katie said. "I remember when Danny had to get six stitches in his forehead. I thought Tommy was going to pass out when he looked at it." Tommy was her husband, also Sharon's brother, and Danny was their adopted son.

"You didn't panic, though, did you?"

"You know what? I didn't and a nurse shouldn't but after it was all over and the stitches were in, I got the worst case of the shakes. It was embarrassing."

GG said, "But understandable. He was your baby."

Katie sighed. "I guess it's true; it's different when it's your own child."

"So what are we celebrating?" GG couldn't wait to find out.

A look of excitement settled on Katie's face. "Well... we

got a visit from Danny and Li last night." She took a sip of her wine, drawing out the suspense.

"Yes? Don't stop there! Tell me."

A huge smile broke out on her face. "They're having a baby!"

GG set her wine down so she could hug her friend close. "Oh, Katie! That's the best news ever! You're going to be a grandma!"

"I know!" She was beaming with joy. "I just can't believe it. They're going to be wonderful parents! You should see Tommy. I think if he could walk down the street telling strangers, he would. He was the best daddy when Danny was little and he can't *wait* to be a grandpa."

When they had calmed down enough, they clinked their glasses together and sipped their wine. Leo was watching them, wondering what they were so excited about, although he suspected he might be able to guess. When he and the girls finished planting all the flowers, he took them inside to wash their hands and then brought them back out along with a fresh plate of cookies.

"Okay, what's going on?" he asked after he kissed Katie on the cheek.

"You'll never guess," said GG.

"Want me to give it a try?"

"No!" Katie exclaimed. "I want to tell you. Danny and Li are having a baby!"

Leo said, "That's what I was going to guess."

"No, you weren't," said GG.

"Honest, I was. What else could put that kind of smile on both your faces?" He had brought out a cold beer for himself and the three of them toasted the unborn baby.

"It's the best news ever," Katie said, her smile never wavering.

"How's Tommy taking it?"

"Oh, my gosh, he's like the only man who ever got the news he was going to be a grandfather. I'll be surprised if the whole county doesn't know by the end of the week."

Leo chuckled. "I'll have to give him a call. Would you ladies like your glasses refilled?"

"Absolutely," said GG.

"I'll do the honors," Leo said and went to the kitchen to get the bottle.

Savannah asked, "What's happening, Gran?"

"Aunt Katie just got some very good news. She's going to be a grandma."

Shelby and Savannah both smiled and Savannah asked, "Just like Gran?"

Katie said, "That's right, just like your gran."

Shelby said, "But it's going to be a little baby, right?"

"That's right, a brand new little human."

Shelby said wistfully, "I wish we had a little baby at our house."

Savannah gave a snort. "I don't. Everybody loves the babies more than anybody else. I like babies, but I like it when they just visit."

Leo came out in time to hear that and all the adults laughed. "You are one of a kind, Savannah."

"No, I'm not, I'm a twin. Look at Shelby, she looks just like me."

GG said, "Yes, she does, but you're still very different from each other."

Savannah thought that over. "Yeah, I guess we are. I'm a lot louder than Shelby."

The adults were laughing again and Shelby said, "She really is."

GG asked, "Does Sharon know?"

"Not yet. She and Jack have been on a mini vacation; she said they needed a break and they'll be back on Friday."

GG said, "I see a girls' night coming up soon."

Katie smiled. "That sounds like a great idea."

"As soon as Sharon gets back, we'll set it up."

"Aunt Katie, Carter broke his arm today," Shelby said.

"I know, your gran told me. That must have been scary."

Savannah said, "Well, it probably was, but Carter says he's not scared of anything. Not even alligators!"

Leo said, "That was a pretty safe thing for him to say, considering the size of the alligator population in Indiana."

They all laughed and Savannah looked mystified. "Huh?"

GG said, "Paw-Paw just means that there aren't any alligators in Indiana, so if Carter says that, nobody's ever going to know if it's really true."

Shelby said, "I will, because I *know* if Carter saw an alligator, he'd be scared."

Savannah nodded. "He would, for real."

Katie was giggling helplessly. "I can't wait to be having these kinds of conversations with my grandkids."

GG promised her solemnly, "It is honestly never boring."

"Where did Jack and Sharon go on their mini vacation?" Leo asked.

"They flew to the Bahamas."

"What's the Bahamas?" asked Shelby.

GG explained, "It's an island in the ocean, with lots of beaches so you can swim and play in the sand."

"Maybe we need a mini vacation," said Leo. "That sounds awfully tempting."

Savannah said, "You should take Carter. Maybe he could see an alligator."

Now GG and Katie were both giggling.

Leo said, "Well, that's a thought. Not quite what I had in mind, though."

"What did you have in mind, Paw-Paw?" Shelby asked.

GG kicked him under the table and he said, "I had in mind a little vacation just for Gran and me."

"Won't you be bored?" asked his granddaughter.

"Nope." Leo shook his head earnestly. "I won't be one bit bored."

"Good answer," said his wife.

"The Bahamas sound lovely," Katie said with a sigh. "Someday we'll get away for a vacation like that."

GG admitted, "It does sound like a great idea. Maybe we'll have to plan it. We haven't had a vacation like that in a very long time."

Leo said, "Let's do it. We'll sit down tomorrow evening and look at the calendar, pick a date, and make some reservations."

"Just like that?" GG asked.

"Just like that. There's no reason in the world why we can't. I have plenty of vacation time stored up at work. We'll tell the kids when they come tomorrow and just let them know when we choose our dates." Leo was fired up at the whole idea.

GG smiled and said, "Let's do it."

Shelby climbed up into GG's lap and asked, "Gran, will you bring me back a shell from the beach? Callie has one and she can hear the *ocean* in it!"

"I sure will. I'll bring both of you a shell."

Savannah said, "Can you bring Carter an alligator?"

GG laughed and said, "No, they won't let me do that. But, if we see an alligator, I'll take a picture of it and give it to you."

"Okay, I bet Carter will even be scared of a picture!"

Soon, Katie said, "I should get going. Tommy and I are going to celebrate the prospect of being grandparents tonight; I'm taking him out."

GG said, "That sounds like fun. Where are you taking him?"

"I'm taking him to his favorite place to have dinner out. Our backyard."

GG laughed and said, "He's not much for going out, is he?"

"Nope. When it comes right down to it, we're both home bodies, so I guess it works for us. We'll have a fire in the pit and fix steaks over the wood fire. All I have to do is make a salad and we've got dinner out."

GG gave her a hug. "It sounds perfect. Give Tommy a hug for us."

"I will." Katie got hugs from all of them, including two from Shelby and went on her way with a happy wave.

"Gosh, that's wonderful news. That's the happiest I've seen her since she and Tommy adopted Danny."

Leo said, "They're going to make great grandparents."

GG nodded her agreement. "Hey, girls, what should we have for dinner tonight? Should we have Paw-Paw make hot dogs on the grill or order pizza?"

"Pizza!" they chorused together.

"Okay, pizza it is." It was their favorite meal and GG hadn't really needed to ask the question.

It was a noisy, happy evening and, after dinner and baths, Shelby insisted on calling to see how Carter was. She felt better after her parents assured her that her big brother was doing fine and even better after he got on the phone and teased her a little, with Savannah getting a chance to talk to him too. The two girls made it upstairs to bed under their own steam, unlike the night before, and by the time they were tucked in, they were already beginning to drift off to sleep.

GG's shop remained closed the following day. Everyone knew to call to check on business hours on Mondays, but she gave Leo a sign to hang on her door on his way to work. It was a cloudy, drizzly day so she and the girls spent the day doing craft projects and GG read to them about Savannah's favorite subject, horses, and Shelby's current favorite, elephants. They made pigs in a blanket for lunch, a dish that always made them giggle, and after lunch, they lay on a blanket on the floor in the den and watched a Disney movie. It was the kind of a day that GG loved and Leo left work a couple of hours early and surprised them in the middle of the afternoon.

"Paw-Paw!" Both girls ran to him and he swept them up in his arms.

"I missed you, so I begged and begged my boss to let me go home early."

Savannah giggled. "You *are* the boss!"

Leo said, "Well, not quite, but they let me leave early anyway."

"What did you bring, Paw-Paw?" Shelby asked, spotting the books he had laid on the hall table.

"I stopped at the library and I got a book full of pictures of the Bahamas, so you can see where Gran and I are going for our vacation. And I got a book about horses and another one about elephants. We don't let rainy days bother us, do we?"

"Nope," Savannah declared. "Rainy days don't bother us!"

GG said, "Let Paw-Paw go change his clothes and then I bet he'll look at those books with you."

Sure enough, a few minutes later, Leo was ensconced on the couch with a twin on each side, and they were engrossed in the books. GG went to start her spaghetti and meatballs while they chattered over the books with their grandpa. James called not long after that and said they were on their way and would be there in a couple of hours.

"We'll all have spaghetti and meatballs while you're here," GG said and heard Carter give a cheer in the background.

When James and Allison came through the front door with Carter, the noise level shot through the roof. Shelby's eyes were huge as she gazed at the cast on his arm and the sling he wore to support it. Even Savannah looked a little worried as she checked out her brother. They crowded close to him, but they were careful not to bump his arm.

"Does it hurt?" asked Shelby.

"Sometimes," Carter said. "But not the way it did when it first happened. Then, it hurt a *lot!*"

Savannah looked awed. "So much that you cried?"

Carter looked scornful. "Boys don't cry."

"I would," Shelby said without hesitation.

James said, "I did when I broke mine. And I was even on the football field."

Carter said sheepishly, "Well, maybe I did… just a little."

"That's okay," Shelby said generously, "I think everybody should cry when they break a bone."

"Look, Carter, we made you something," said Savannah.

Excitedly, the girls presented the cards GG had helped them make for their brother. He grinned at them, genuinely pleased.

"These are cool! Look, Mom, they *made* these. I'm going to put them on the dresser in my room."

The girls were overcome with pride at his reaction and they chattered with him and showed him the books they'd been looking at. "Look, Carter, this is where Gran and Paw-Paw are going to go."

"Wow, it's the ocean and the beach."

Allison looked up, curious. "Are you two going on vacation?"

GG said, "Yeah, it was kind of a spur of the moment decision, but we decided, why not?"

"The Bahamas! You're going to love it; it's about time you took some time for yourselves." Allison beamed at them.

James said, "Yeah, but I am so jealous right now. The sand, the sun, pina coladas; it sounds like heaven."

Savannah said, "Yeah, but there aren't any alligators."

It took them all by surprise and then they burst out laughing. Allison said, "I'd say that's a good thing."

They had a delicious family dinner together and, not long after, the kids had to be on their way home. There were hugs and kisses all around and James and Allison thanked them again for everything.

"Just stop," GG said. "We always love having the kids here. Carter, you take care of that arm and no climbing trees in a cast."

Carter laughed. "I promise."

GG and Leo stood in the driveway, waving and watching until they were out of sight. Leo put his arm around his wife and she sighed happily as they turned to go back inside.

"We really have a great family, don't we?" she asked.

Leo kissed her. "We sure do. Now, let's go plan that vacation."

GG squealed when he gave her a little swat on the butt as they walked through the door.

Chapter 3

Leo and GG stood on their little balcony and gazed out over the white, sandy beach extending down to the blue, blue water. They had opted not to be on the ground floor, even though they could have walked right out onto the beach, in favor of the quieter privacy of a third story room. It was an adults only accommodation and it was meant for lovers. They had just arrived a short time ago and were completely pleased with their small suite and found a bottle of champagne already chilling in an ice bucket, along with a basket of fruit, cheeses, and crackers. There were fresh flowers and a fragrant, ocean-scented breeze wafting in through the terrace doors.

"Oh, Leo, this is just beautiful," GG said with a sigh.

"Almost as beautiful as you," he said, capturing her mouth with his.

"What took us so long to do something like this?" she murmured against his mouth.

"Slow learners?" He chuckled at her. "Champagne, Mrs. Beauchamp?"

"Oh, yes, Mr. Beauchamp."

He popped the cork and poured the bubbly while GG kicked off her shoes and breathed deep in the ocean breeze. They sipped the delicious wine and toasted each other and then wrapped their arms around each other and turned, lips locked together, in a slow spin of love. The kiss was deep and dreamy, tasting of champagne and strawberries, leaving them breathless with the embers of desire that it awoke. Leo buried a hand in her hair and kissed her eyelids with feathery, little touches and then trailed a line of burning kisses down the side of her face and to her throat. She was nearly purring with the pleasure of his touch and her head fell back to expose the line of her throat for his mouth.

"Leo," she whispered, "I love you so much."

"Not any more than I love you," he murmured back, kissing the hollow of her collarbone. He nibbled at the base of her throat and a shiver crawled down her spine, making her arch her back with the sensation that made her quiver and made her nipples tighten in a delicious reaction to his touch.

Leo put her glass to her lips and she drank, her eyes fastened on him, dark and heavy with desire. He undid the buttons of her gauzy white top and stroked the tops of her breasts above the lacy white bra that teased him with its hints of the beauty that it hid. He could see the rosy tips that pressed against the lace and he ached for her, already hard and ready. He slid the top down over her shoulders and it fluttered to the floor, followed by the wisp of lace. He stepped back and gazed at her, drinking in the sight of her bare breasts, and his rigid member strained against the constraints of his clothing. He burned with need, his cock aching and raging with the intensity of his desire. GG could read him and she reached for his belt, unbuckling it and undoing his pants to set him free. He groaned as she pushed his pants down and his manhood sprang to attention. He needed her naked under his hands and he made short work of undressing her until they stood, wrapped in each other's' arms, with nothing but skin between them.

Leo's hands wandered over her, stroking, kneading, cupping her heavy breasts and teasing the swollen tips with gentle pinches. She quivered with the tremors of desire, the shivers that ran up and down her spine and weakened her knees. There was a little, wordless moan from the back of her throat and the heat rippled between her thighs as she felt the juices gather there when he cupped her buttocks in his hands and pulled her against him, trapping his rigid member between them. GG gasped and the room spun around her, the light dimming until she felt she was spinning in some kind of maelstrom where there was only sensation, wild arousal that consumed her and swept her into the storm. She felt the heat between them, growing until it shot into a raging inferno and engulfed them both.

Her hands reached for him and she closed them around his shaft, marveling at the size of him and greedily stroking and squeezing it until he gave a hoarse cry and thrust his hand between her legs. His fingers explored her swollen folds and her knees gave way beneath her so that he had to catch her and carry her to the bed. He closed his mouth over one turgid, swollen teat and she arched her back as he pushed a finger into her tight, hot center, making her cry out as he added another. She gripped him in her hand and squeezed, stroking the full length of him and pulling at him before she slid her hand down to cup and squeeze his balls, wringing a groan from him.

The intensity of their passion burned hotter and hotter and they were lost in a flood of sensation, carried away on waves of pleasure until they had to be one together and Leo spread her legs to meet his hard, savage thrust. She thrust herself up to meet him and they ground together, his cock buried in her. For a moment, they couldn't move and then he pulled back and plunged into her again, desperate to have all of her. She rose to meet him and their bodies slammed together frantically, rocking in a hard, fast rhythm as the flame inside them rose higher. GG was crying out with each thrust, grinding her hips against him as her need grew, and Leo bit back a shout as he knew he was going to come, and there was no stopping it. GG felt herself shooting up and up until the climax shook her with savage force and her muscles spasmed in hard contractions until Leo couldn't hold back another second and he came, emptying himself with deep, throbbing shudders as her muscles contracted around him. They lay there together, rocked with shudders and quivers of pleasure, aftershocks that slowly died, leaving them utterly spent.

It was several minutes before either of them could speak. GG said, "If this is a mini vacation, we should have done it a long time ago."

"We won't make that mistake again. Vacations are going to be a regular part of our lives from now on."

GG laughed weakly. "Did you ever think we'd be like this at this age?"

"Absolutely. And what do you mean, at this age? We're not old, for heaven's sake. But, personally, I plan to be like this when we're seventy."

GG laughed again. "I really don't want to think about being seventy yet."

"I do. I'm looking forward to being old together, watching our grandchildren and great grandchildren grow up, seeing them graduate and get married. I'm looking forward to sitting on the porch with you and still pinching your butt when you walk by. I'm looking forward to getting crotchety and getting away with it. I'm looking forward to telling stories to our great grandchildren. It's all a blessing."

GG had tears in her eyes. "Oh, Leo, how did I ever get lucky enough to marry you?"

He held her tight and said, "We were lucky, both of us. We were meant to be together for the rest of our lives."

They never left their room that first day of their vacation. They plundered the basket of fruit and found a selection of sausages to go along with the cheese and crackers so they ordered another bottle of wine and fed each other grapes and strawberries and they made love again while the pink and orange glow of the sunset over the water shone through their terrace doors, this time slowly and tenderly, with lingering touches and whispers of love. They soaked in a mountain of bubbles in the big tub and then dressed in the luxurious bathrobes provided by the hotel and ordered a decadent dessert and nightcaps of brandy.

They didn't spend their whole vacation making love; they walked on the beach, waded in the warm water, went out on a catamaran, took a scuba diving lesson, and spent a day shopping in the market in town. GG found shells for the girls and bought souvenirs for the whole family. When it was over and they flew back home, they were relaxed and happy, rejuvenated and more in love than ever. They promised each other that they would have a vacation every year, just the two of them and even their everyday life back in Boone seemed to have a new spark to it.

A couple of weeks after they got back from their vacation, GG got a call from her brother, Bryce. "GG, I'm coming home for a vacation," he told her.

"Really? A real vacation? When? That's such good news!"

He laughed at her. "I'll be there two weeks from Sunday. I hope you're going to be around."

"Of course, we are! How long will you be here?"

"I have two whole weeks. I'll have a day of travel each way, but that's still twelve days of vacation time."

"Oh, Bryce, I can't wait! And you'll stay with us; we have plenty of room."

"So where are Mom and Dad right now?"

"They're on their way to Virginia to meet up with some of their camping friends. That's this weekend. I'll call Mom and I'm sure they'll be here when you get here."

"Good. I can't wait to see you all; it seems like it's been forever."

"It has been a long time. But twelve whole days! We never get you for that long. Oh, did you hear the news about Danny and Li?"

"No, what's the news?"

"They're going to have a baby! Bryce, you're going to be a grandpa, kind of."

Bryce actually got a little choked up. He cleared his throat and said gruffly, "That really *is* good news. I talk to Danny about once a month. I won't let on that I heard about it."

"Good, he'll want to tell you himself, I'm sure."

"He's a good kid. Quyen would have been proud of him."

Quyen had died giving birth to Danny and he'd been left an orphan in a strange country. Bryce had married Quyen to get her out of Vietnam after her family had disowned her for falling in love with an American GI and getting pregnant. Katie and Tommy had adopted the baby boy, and once he'd gotten old enough, he and Bryce had connected and stayed in contact with each other ever since. Danny called Bryce his bonus father and they had always shared the bond of Quyen.

GG said, "He still visits her grave regularly."

"Like I said, he's a good kid. Well, I should get off the phone. I'll see you two weeks from Sunday."

GG was beaming when she hung up. She called her mom and Margo cried when she heard the news. "Of course, we'll be there! We can park at your place, right?"

"Yep, just like always."

"We're overdue for a visit to Boone anyway and now it's

going to be even better. Oh, here comes Don, I have to tell him. I'll talk to you soon, honey. Love you!"

GG was chuckling when she hung up. When Leo walked in that night, he could immediately smell his favorite dinner cooking.

"What's the occasion?" he asked, kissing his wife.

She grinned at him. "Bryce is coming home!"

Leo looked shocked. "To stay?"

"No, of course not, but for two whole weeks. He's getting a real vacation."

Leo looked thrilled. "That's great, baby. It'll be good to see him; it seems like it's been a long time."

"That's what I told him. And Mom and Dad are coming; I told them they could park here."

Leo nodded. "Of course, that's why I put that hookup in. I wouldn't let them stay anywhere else."

GG gave him another kiss and then handed him a beer. "Dinner will be ready in half an hour or so."

The time alternately dragged and flew before the big weekend. GG's parents pulled in on Saturday and they had a noisy reunion with a fair amount of tears and laughter. James and his family would be there in the morning and Carl and his wife were coming around lunchtime. It was going to be just the kind of family-filled house that GG loved most. GG had fixed a huge tray of cold cuts and cheeses for sandwiches and she had bowls full of assorted salads to go with them. She'd baked cookies and brownies and had a pan of baked beans and one of baked macaroni and cheese. Bryce had called from the airport in Indianapolis and by the time Carl got there, Bryce was due within the hour. GG had set out a big tray of fresh vegetables with dip to snack on and she and Margo had decided to wait until Bryce arrived to get everything else out.

Suddenly they could hear a horn blaring outside and Leo

and Carl threw open the front door to see a car pulling into the driveway.

"Holy shit, look what he's driving," Carl said with a whistle.

"Wow, I hope he gives us a chance to drive that," Leo responded.

Then the entire place erupted into happy chaos as Bryce climbed out of the fancy sports car and grinned at them all. "Now, this is a greeting!" he exclaimed and then it was all just a jumble of noise.

It was a solid ten minutes before the excitement calmed enough for them to begin talking to each other. Bryce had a little girl on each hip and Carter was right beside them. The men and kids had gone out to the backyard while the ladies got the lunch spread all arranged on the long kitchen island. When they were ready, Margot called them all in and Don said a prayer of thanks for all of the family's blessings. Margot and GG both shed a few happy tears at the warmth of having the whole family gathered together. Then they all filled their plates. There were lots of lawn chairs out back and the bench seats around the edge of the deck as well, so they all went outside to eat. The weather was perfect and Leo and Don had filled coolers with sodas, water, and beer, all iced down. Bryce told stories about his adventures, as he always did, and kept everyone laughing.

"Now, Bryce," said Margot. "You didn't come to drop some bombshell on us about your next dangerous assignment, did you?"

Bryce laughed. "No, not this time, Mom. Things are pretty calm right now. My next assignment is actually going to be to cover a humanitarian effort to bring clean water to some places in Africa and to open some schools in those same places. Pretty tame stuff."

Margot laid her hand on her heart. "Thank the Lord!"

They all laughed at her, but Bryce had spent years covering some of the most dangerous stories in the world. None of them would ever forget the visit he had made home to tell them that he was going to Saigon to cover the Vietnam war. And he had survived it, as he had each dangerous assignment that had been made to him during the years after that. It would be a relief to see him cover a place where bombs wouldn't be falling.

GG asked, "So why the change?"

Bryce shrugged a little and said, "There was nothing that was pulling at me, urging me to go cover it. They asked me to go to Nigeria and it just didn't seem right, so I turned it down. I don't know, maybe I'm slowing down a little."

GG studied him and suggested, "Maybe it's time to have something more in your life than the story?"

"Hey, I always said keep it light, no serious attachments, and I've been just fine with that."

"Yeah?"

"And maybe… maybe it's time for a change."

His sister smiled quietly at him. She hoped it was true; she would love for him to have a love interest in his life. He'd been happy chasing the stories and the adventures for a lot of years, but she still would be thrilled to see him happily in love. There was a shout from the side gate and GG looked over to see Katie and Tommy, with Danny and his wife, Li, behind them.

"Come on in!" Leo called, hurrying over to greet them. Tommy was carrying a cooler and Katie had a big, covered dish, while Li held a basket of fresh fruit.

More greetings were exchanged and Bryce had a big bearhug for Danny and then a warm hug for Li, whom he was meeting for the first time.

"You didn't have to bring anything," GG told Katie as she hugged her. "But what is it?"

Katie lifted the foil cover a little and let her peek.

"Oh, Katie! It's your homemade fried chicken! The best we've ever tasted. Let's take it in and put it with the rest of the food. We can get the first crack at it that way." Laughing, they carried the chicken into the house and Li surrendered the basket of fruit.

The feasting and conversation went on through the day and into the evening until James and Allison decided they needed to start home with their tired girls. They said their goodbyes and went on their way, but the adults stayed on, talking and snacking until the hour was late. The food had been put away some time ago and they had all pitched in to clean up the kitchen, so they were free to talk as long as they wanted to. The men had all checked out the sports car Bryce had rented and he promised them all a chance to drive it. It was a close-knit group, even though it wasn't often that they all got together and they thoroughly enjoyed catching up with each other. Finally, they had to give in to the yawns that were taking over and Carl and Peggy left, promising to be back again, followed soon after by Tommy and Katie with Danny and Li.

Don and Margo retired to their home on wheels and Bryce and GG and Leo all went upstairs. Soon the house was dark and quiet.

Chapter 4

The time of Bryce's visit went by too quickly, but they fit a lot into it. He came to see GG's shop and went out to dinner with Danny and Li. He and Carl spent a day fishing together, topped off with burgers and fries at the Burger Barn. Margot and GG went with him to visit Quyen's grave and GG and Leo's stillborn son, from GG's first pregnancy that had ended in such heartbreak. He spent a day just with GG, riding around in the fancy sports car to all the places around Boone that had been a part of their lives since they were born, just talking about everything. GG took him to the VA hospital and introduced him to Mac, who still worked there. He spent a couple of days on his own, connecting with old buddies and schoolmates. It was the most time he'd spent at home in years and it did him good. At the end of his vacation time, he could honestly say he'd had real time with all the people he loved and he felt renewed and ready for the next chapter in his life.

When he had to leave, GG was sad, but she was enormously grateful for all the time they'd had together. He drove himself to the airport so that he could say goodbye to everyone at home, not in the sterile atmosphere of the airport. So he had one of his mom's home cooked breakfasts before he left Boone and he appreciated every bite of it. He hugged them all and took an envelope full of photos back with him, promising to call GG as soon as he arrived at his destination in Africa. And GG and Margot cried in each other's arms after he pulled out of the driveway and honked the horn as he left.

Bryce wasn't due to travel to Africa for a few days after he got back to London, so Don and Margot decided to get back to their itinerary for the summer and said their goodbyes a couple of days after Bryce had left. GG hated to see them go, but they were having so much fun traveling around and meeting up with friends, she couldn't begrudge them their retirement fun. She got a text finally that told her Bryce would be on a flight to Africa in another two days and she waited to hear from him after his arrival. She finally got the call, with Bryce laughing and letting her know that he'd arrived safe and sound and would be in touch soon.

The next time he called, Bryce was full of enthusiastic stories about the work that the organization was doing there to help the people build clean water resources and to build and run schools for the children who had no educational system. He had met a woman who was instrumental in seeing that these schools got built, that children got to attend them. He sounded as if he was full of admiration for her and he was excited about helping her. He wrote pieces that were published in western countries, where there were possible donors who could help further her work.

"He's so excited about everything he's doing over there," GG said, reading Bryce's latest letter that included excerpts from his Time Magazine piece. "I think he's really found something special. And I think that maybe this woman is special to him too."

"Really?" Leo asked. "He really did sound like he was ready for some changes when he was here, didn't he?"

"He did. He even said maybe it was time to have someone special in his life."

"He said that?"

"Yeah. He was kind of talking only to me, but he said it."

"He's a good man," Leo said. "He's done a lot of amazing work."

GG sighed and said, "It's so strange, when I think back to when he was still in school and everything was about sports and cars and girls. I never thought he'd end up being an important journalist."

"Pretty cool, huh?"

"Yeah, it really is." GG snuggled closer to her husband and he kissed her on the top of the head.

The family hoped for another visit from Bryce for Christmas, but it turned out that he couldn't come. There was some unrest in the country he was working in and it just wasn't practical or safe to try to go home. He spent the holidays in a school for children who had never seen a Christmas present in their lives, but that Christmas they did. Margaret Chase, the woman in charge of the schools, did everything humanly possible to see that there was a Christmas tree, treats, and little gifts of books and shoes for each of the children. And Bryce helped her with every step of it. On Christmas Eve, after the children slept, Bryce and Margaret toasted each other with a bottle of decent if not excellent whiskey and then they made love until the darkest part of the night, when they fell asleep in each other's arms.

Christmas in Indiana was as it always was, with family and friends and a table groaning with its load of delicious food. The children had the most fun, although the adults had nearly as much, just from watching them. Bryce was able to call and wish them all a merry Christmas and everyone shouted their love to him.

After his phone call, Bryce and Margaret sang traditional songs with the school children until they had their Christmas dinner that included a fat goat that they roasted on a spit over a fire. Bryce saw a future stretching ahead of him that held much more promise than anything he'd ever seen before. He was content, the restlessness that had always clawed at him was stilled and he was content with the path he saw.

GG stood holding the phone for a minute after the call ended. Leo came over and took it out of her hand and hung it up. "What is it?" he asked.

"I don't know. He sounded different."

"Different how?"

GG struggled to explain. "I'm not sure, but he was calm. He's usually kind of excited all the time. This time, he was just… peaceful, I guess would be the right word."

"That's good, isn't it?" Leo asked.

"Yeah, I think he's sort of content, maybe, or happy."

Leo kissed her and said, "Then that is good."

She smiled at him and said, "Yes. Maybe he's found that extra something in his life."

Leo winked at her and said, "Let's hope so."

"I'd like it if he'd settle down a little with someone he loves."

"There's that matchmaking tendency trying to come out again. Come on, the girls have a couple more presents to open. And I think I'd better help James keep Carter from trying out that football in the house."

GG laughed and went back to the merriment with him. Margot was sitting with her great-granddaughters, helping them comb the manes and tails of their new "little ponies" and Carter was wheedling his dad to go outside and throw the football with him.

James groaned, "Son, there's six inches of snow out there!"

"Yeah, Dad, it'll be cool. There's snow on real football fields, right?"

Leo laughed at them. "Yeah, Dad, it'll be cool. Literally."

James scowled at him and said, "You're not helping, Dad."

Don came to the rescue, handing over an unopened gift. "Look, we missed one for Carter."

Carter took it eagerly, examining the tag on it. "Hey, it's from Uncle Bryce!"

Margot said, "And here are the girls' gifts from Uncle Bryce, all the way from Africa."

Carter opened his gift and looked at the finely crafted wooden item. "What is it?"

Don said, "Look, it opens like this. It's called Mancala and it's a game of strategy. If we go over to the table, I can show you how to play. Later, you can learn other ways that you can play; there are lots of variations. It's a two-person game. This mancala board was handmade in Africa. It's beautiful, isn't it, Margot?"

"It really is."

"Should we try it?" Don asked.

Carter was fascinated. "Sure! Are these the game pieces, these little stones?"

"That's right." The two of them moved over to the table and Carter was soon engrossed in learning about the game.

Margot handed a small package to each of the girls and told them, "These are from Uncle Bryce."

Shelby looked at hers reverently. "I never had a present from another country before."

GG said, "It's going to be a special one." She was wearing the necklace Bryce had sent to her, made of hand carved wooden beads with an unusual carved pendant in the center.

Shelby and Savannah opened the packages and their eyes widened as they saw the brightly colored bead bracelets.

"Gran, look!" Savannah exclaimed.

"It's so pretty!" Shelby said. "Do girls in Africa wear these?"

GG said, "I'm sure they do. Here, let me help you with them." She helped them put the bracelets on, marveling at the thought of the wonders Bryce was experiencing, the things he was seeing that were so different from what she knew.

Allison exclaimed over the bracelets and the girls proudly skipped around the room, showing them off to everyone. And so Bryce had made his presence felt on Christmas, even though he was so far away. Carl and Peggy had stopped by on Christmas Eve to wish everyone a merry Christmas, but they had been busy with their own extended family on Christmas Day. And GG and Leo had kept their Christmas Eve tradition, along with GG's parents, of attending the Christmas Eve candlelight service at the little church in Boone at the hour before midnight. It was always hauntingly lovely and they had only missed one Christmas Eve service in all the years they'd been married.

Leo and James were turning on the football game in the den and GG, Margot, and Allison were enjoying a glass of wine while the girls watched The Little Mermaid for the millionth time. Don and Carter were still engrossed in their game and kept at it until they could hear the football game getting exciting. Carter carefully put all the little stones away in the leather pouch they'd come in and closed the hinged board. Don got himself a beer and went to join the other two men and Carter followed him after he convinced his mom that he should be able to have a Coke on Christmas. Later, they snacked on leftovers from Christmas dinner and stuffed themselves all over again. Allison and James and the kids were spending the night, another Christmas tradition.

"When is Katie's new grandbaby due?" Margot asked.

"January tenth," GG said with a beaming smile. "She can't

wait. They're having a boy and Tommy's planning his first car."

Margot and Allison laughed and Allison said, "I think my dad would have been like that if we'd known Carter was going to be a boy."

Margot said, "You knew pretty early that you were carrying twins, didn't you, sweetie?"

Allison nodded. "I did. So I had plenty of excuses to take it easy and let James wait on me."

They all laughed, remembering how anxious James had been during the pregnancy.

"Mom, you didn't know about the boys, right?" GG asked.

"That's right, we didn't find out until almost the very end. So I felt like an elephant all that time without a good excuse. You should have seen your dad's face when the doctor said there were two heartbeats. He didn't know whether to faint with shock or burst with pride."

"And James," Allison said, knowing the story well, "you didn't even suspect you were carrying him for a long time, did you?"

GG shook her head. "Nope. I thought I just gained a few pounds because of the holidays. Doc Harper said I didn't want to know because I would have been too scared, so I just didn't recognize any of the signs."

Allison squeezed her hand.

"When I finally realized it, my words to Leo were, 'I think something happened.' And he said, 'I know.' I was never so shocked in my life! And scared, so we decided to keep it to ourselves for as long as possible."

"They avoided seeing us for weeks," said Margot, "and when they finally invited us over for dinner, she was almost seven months pregnant. I felt James move the same day I found out he was coming."

GG said, "It was normal to be scared, after everything

we'd been through, but honestly, the pregnancy was nothing like anything I'd experienced before. I felt great, everyone said I looked good, it all just felt normal and healthy. And there wasn't a bit of trouble through the pregnancy or the delivery."

Allison's eyes shone. "It was meant to be."

"It was. And now, just look at this family."

"And we have great-grandchildren!" Margot said happily.

Allison asked, "How did you feel when you found out that was coming?"

Margot laughed. "For five minutes I felt like the oldest woman in the world. Then I thought, a baby's coming! And it was great from that moment on. There's great freedom in being a great-grandma. You can do pretty much anything you want, say what you want, and enjoy the kids with none of the worries of being parents. It's like that being a grandparent too, but even more when you're a great-grandparent."

Leo came in after more beer, kissing GG on his way to the refrigerator and popping a bite of turkey into his mouth. "What are we talking about, ladies?"

GG smiled sweetly at him and said, "Pregnancy."

He grabbed a piece of ham and said, "Gotta get back to the game." Their laughter followed him out of the kitchen.

Margot asked, "When are Jack and Sharon going to get to be grandparents?"

"Believe me, they're asking the same thing. But all their kids followed their parents' examples and they want to finish college first and get their careers started before they have babies. Jack Jr. is the only one left in college now, so hopefully soon. Sharon's worried about having wrinkles before she has a grandbaby." GG had to laugh at her friend.

"She'll forget all about it when the first one comes," Margot said.

"That's what I told her. Who cares about wrinkles when you're holding a baby?"

Allison said, "She always looks so great I'll bet she'll be ninety before she has a wrinkle."

They looked over as the movie ended and saw both girls sound asleep on the couch. GG shrugged and started the movie over again. "That way, they won't wake up when it stops."

Allison said, "I use that trick too."

"I know, I learned it from you." GG topped off their glasses and nibbled at a piece of cheese.

Allison said, "Naps don't happen that often anymore, so I don't like to cut them short. In the fall, they'll start school."

GG and Margot both shook their heads. Margot said, "That's so hard to believe."

"I know."

GG looked at her speculatively. "Well, you could always have another one."

Allison looked shocked. "No! That is definitely not in the plans. We always planned on two kids and look what happened. We have the perfect family now and it's not going to expand."

GG was laughing. "I know, but I had to tease you a little. Although, I wouldn't mind it."

"Mm hm. You'll have to wait for great-grandbabies."

GG grew serious. "Honestly, I can't argue with you; you have the perfect family and I consider us to be so lucky, it's hard to even express it."

"Aww." Allison hugged her mother-in-law hard.

Margot said, "Speaking of kids growing up too fast, look at Carter! He's really shot up this year."

"I know, I had to get him all new school clothes for the second semester; he's already growing out of everything I bought him at the end of the summer."

"I had the same problem with Leo," GG said thoughtfully. The others stared at her and then burst out laughing.

GG grinned and said, "We were getting a little too serious."

The men came in from the den and Leo said, "It's half-time. We need sustenance."

"Dig right in, it's all right here and the microwave is empty." GG had done her kitchen duty for the day; they were on their own for leftovers.

When they left the room a few minutes later, they had fully loaded plates, even Carter. Margot shook her head and said, "Can you believe the way they can eat?"

Allison said, "No, it's shocking. I think I'll make a little sandwich with turkey and one of those rolls."

GG said, "Good idea. I think my stomach just growled. And that pecan pie looks really tempting."

In a few minutes, they were settled at the table with their own plates and the girls woke up halfway through the second running of The Little Mermaid. Allison let them choose what they wanted to eat, as long as it wasn't all dessert and they settled down happily behind TV trays to finish the movie. It was a wonderful Christmas and when the adults finally called it a night, the house settled around them and they all slept soundly with happy hearts.

Chapter 5

It was springtime, finally, after an unusually cold winter, and it seemed that everyone in Boone had a touch of cabin fever. It wasn't quite nice enough yet to enjoy the outdoors, but it was easy to see that it would be soon. GG and Leo were planning to take their next vacation in the dead of winter so that they could get a real break from cold, dreary weather. They had agreed that, although the beach was great anytime they went, it would be even better in the middle of winter. The highlight of the entire winter had been the arrival of Katie and Tommy's new grandson.

GG and Sharon had rushed to the hospital to wait with Katie when Li had gone into labor. It turned out to be an easy delivery, and the healthy, seven-pound little boy was born after only seven hours of labor. He was a beautiful baby with lots of silky, black hair and huge, dark, nearly black eyes. They named him Michael Binh Calder, giving him the middle name in honor of his Vietnamese heritage. The three women stood at the glass, looking in at the baby, who was looking solemnly about the room.

GG said, "Oh my gosh, Katie, he's absolutely beautiful!"

Sharon agreed with her and Katie beamed with happiness, gazing at the tiny baby. She had already held him for the first time and was overwhelmed with love. Her life had just become infinitely richer with the new addition to the family. Tommy had held him too, and when the baby had curled his tiny fingers around Tommy's big one, he had completely taken over his grandpa's heart. So that event was the undisputed highlight of the whole winter.

After a lot of discussion, GG and Leo had decided that GG's shop needed a new home. She had outgrown the little space that was GG's Gems and desperately needed a larger one. There was a building for sale right on the main street through the center of Boone, and even though it consisted of two retail spaces, they had put an offer on it and bought it. They had freshened it up with paint and new lighting and GG had found vintage and antique pieces of furniture to serve as display shelves. She was planning a grand opening at the end of May and was nearly finished moving in. It turned out that her old shop was exactly what another woman was looking for, to set up a secondhand bookstore and she bought it from GG as soon as the sign went up in the window. And she rented the other half of her new building to a woman who had dreams of running a bakery. So, in spite of the cold weather, the winter had been a busy time and spring was bringing lots of changes.

GG was working busily in the new shop. She had just begun to unpack her inventory; it was going to be the most fun part of the move, deciding how to display everything. She had a couple of new artists who would have work consigned to her and she was terribly excited about the upcoming grand opening. She had found a beautiful, vintage cash register to do her business on and she had refinished an old sideboard to serve as her counter. Leo had made some changes to the back of it so that she could use it effectively and still have the front of it facing into the shop. The shop had wooden floors, and outside there was a wide, covered front porch that extended all the way across the front of the building. It was a perfect fit in the rustic business area of Boone. Leo had made the sign that was over the door and GG had painted it. It was covered by a tarp for the time being and wouldn't be unveiled until the opening.

The baker was having her ovens installed and she was planning to have her grand opening at the same time as GG's. It was going to be the biggest event Boone had seen since the trail riders' association had held a wagon train event that passed through the town. There were fliers hanging in all the other local shops and offices advertising the openings and it was a constant topic of conversation in the little town. Nobody had been allowed into either of the new businesses since work had begun on them, so the speculation was rampant about what they would look like. Even Sharon and Katie hadn't seen the inside of GG's new shop. Katie had tried to bribe GG with extra baby time but GG hadn't given in.

The days seemed to pass faster and faster as the opening date got closer, and GG had several panic attacks, worrying about not getting done on time. Leo did his best to keep her head clear and he helped her with everything he could. But one afternoon, he walked into the shop to find his wife sitting on the floor right in the middle of the shop, weeping hopelessly.

He rushed to her, panicked, and said, "GG, what happened? Did you fall? Are you all right?"

GG burst into fresh tears. "Oh, Leo, I'm never going to be ready for this! I can't get anything right and I don't know what I'm going to do!"

"Damn it! I thought you were hurt."

More tears poured out. "Everything is such a mess and I don't even know where to start. I've never felt so disorganized in my life."

"GG, look at me. Did you eat lunch today?"

"N-no, I don't even know what time it is."

"Did you eat a good breakfast this morning?"

"I had toast and coffee."

Leo gave her a stern look. "Toast and coffee does not constitute a good breakfast. And it's three thirty in the afternoon. Get up and go wash your face. We're going home and you're going to have a good meal and some rest."

She looked at him as if he'd grown a second head. "Are you crazy? I can't go home now, I've got to take care of this."

"You've got to take care of *you.* This is not the first time you've had this issue and I thought we had an agreement that you are expected to take care of yourself. Isn't that right?"

She looked like a teenager again with her lower lip stuck out. "Yes, but—"

"But nothing. Now let's go. We'll discuss this further at home after you've eaten."

"Leo, I have to—"

"GG, do you want to have that discussion right here and now?"

"No! No, all right, I'm coming." Still pouting, she got up from the floor and went to the little bathroom to splash some cool water on her face.

"I'll follow you," Leo said, waiting for her to lock the shop.

She opened her mouth, took a look at his face, and then closed it again. She hoped she was wrong, but she knew just what kind of "discussion" her husband had in mind. She scolded herself mentally all the way home, wondering why she hadn't just at least packed herself a sandwich to eat while she worked. He was right, not eating when she needed to was the quickest way for her to end up in the state he'd found her. It would have been simple to just make sure that she fixed herself a simple sandwich and then she wouldn't be in the predicament she was in now. She didn't rush home but kept her speed at exactly the speed limit, wishing the drive was a little longer.

Leo pulled into the driveway behind her and took her arm, marching up the front steps and onto the porch without speaking. When they got inside the house, GG hung their jackets up and meekly followed him to the kitchen. Leo took out a plate and loaded it with leftovers from dinner the night before, meatloaf, mashed potatoes, peas and carrots. When the smells began to waft from the microwave, GG's stomach growled loudly and her cheeks turned pink. Her husband set the plate on the table and gestured for her to sit down while he poured her a glass of milk. She ate quietly and had to admit to herself that it was the best tasting meal she'd had in a while. Once she was more than halfway done, she tried speaking to Leo.

"I'm sorry, Leo, I just wasn't thinking. I was so involved with what I was doing. I was going to take a sandwich with me, but I got in a hurry."

"So you ended up with such a drop in your blood sugar that you didn't get much of anything accomplished. Did you have a headache too?"

"Yes, a little bit." She couldn't look him in the eye.

"Well, we've talked about this more than once, haven't we?"

"Yes, but—"

He was shaking his head. "No buts. This time, we're going to make sure that you remember from now on. Finish eating."

She drew it out as long as she could, finishing up when she could see that he was losing patience. It had been a long time since he'd had reason to be stern with her, but he certainly was now. GG took her dishes to the sink and rinsed them, then put them in the dishwasher and turned to see that Leo had pushed his chair clear of the table and was sitting there waiting for her.

"Come here," he said firmly.

GG's stomach crawled with dread and she moved slowly over to stand in front of him. He took her hands and looked up at her.

"You know what comes now?" he asked.

"I don't... I really am sorry, Leo. I promise I won't let it happen again."

"I'm glad that you're sorry, but that's not enough. What happens when you go without eating for too long?"

She hung her head and said, "I can't think straight and everything I try to do goes wrong."

"And what else?"

"I get jittery and I get a headache."

"That's right. And then your day is ruined and *my* day is ruined because it hurts me to see you like that. When I can see how much your head hurts, I can't stand it."

She looked up hopefully. "Well, then, you wouldn't want to hurt my butt now, right?"

He actually laughed. "This is going to be a lesson and a reminder that you won't forget. This is the kind of hurt that will do you good. Now, over here."

He pointed to his lap and she reluctantly moved to stand beside him so he could pull her across his knees. Without any further talk, he raised his arm and brought his hand down on her bottom with a hard, stinging smack. He followed it with three more quick slaps in the same spot, making her cry out in protest. Then he turned to the other cheek and was soon peppering her bottom with sharp smacks, all over both cheeks. He stopped to pull up her skirt and tug down her panties and the spanking continued. He spanked her harder and harder and aimed his slaps progressively lower on her bottom until he reached the tender spot where her butt met her thigh. GG was howling at the burning pain, squirming and kicking frantically, trying to get away from his brutally hard hand.

"Ow, ow, ow!" she wailed, "I'm sorry, I really am! Please stop, Leo, please!"

But the spanking went on for several more hard smacks before he stopped, laying his hand on her flaming bottom and feeling the heat rise off her flesh. "Now, GG, you're going to get up and take off your skirt. And then you're going to go over there to the drawer and get your paddle and bring it to me."

"Nooo," GG wailed. He immediately delivered several hard smacks to her sit spot and she gasped. "All right! All right, I'll do it."

Leo helped her stand up and she slowly unzipped her skirt and took it off, folding it carefully. She stood there, naked from the waist down and looking pitifully at him. He motioned toward the drawer and tears came to her eyes as she turned and walked slowly over to open it and take out the paddle that was kept there. She brought it back to him and held it out reluctantly. She was back over his lap in a second, and this time, he pinned her hands together at the small of her back, holding them firmly with his left hand while he laid the cool, smooth, wooden paddle against her reddened cheeks. He drew it slowly across her bottom, raised it high and brought it down with a sharp crack.

GG kicked and wailed and begged as her husband paddled her mercilessly, determined that he would never have to do it again, at least not for this reason. Her bottom was on fire, burning and throbbing until she finally burst into tears, sobbing and slowing her struggles until she lay limp across his lap, accepting the cracks of the paddle. There were just a few more and then he stopped. He gathered her up and held her on his lap, letting her cry it out on his shoulder.

"I'd much rather do this in playtime, not punishment," he said ruefully. "Please don't make me do it again."

"I'd rather do it in playtime too," GG muttered with a

hiccup as her tears began to dry. And yet, she felt better, as if the pressure had been lifted off her. She lifted her face and Leo kissed her.

"Do you feel better now?" he asked.

"I felt better right after I ate. But yes! Yes, I do feel better. I should go and get some things done now that I can think straight."

But Leo was shaking his head. "No, you're not going anywhere. You're going to get a good night's sleep, and in the morning you're going to eat a real breakfast and then you're going to fix a lunch to take to the shop with you. Understood?"

"Yes, you're right," she said meekly. She laid her head on his shoulder and her arms slid around him. "But, Leo, it's early…"

"Yes? I suppose it is."

"So, that means there's time for—"

He raised his eyebrows. "Time for what?"

"Well, time for a little cuddling, maybe a little… makeup sex?"

He let out a laugh and said, "That's actually a good idea. As long as you take this seriously; you *have* to take care of yourself."

"I will, Leo, I promise."

As they started up the stairs, Leo gave her a sharp swat on her red bottom and made her squeal and grab her cheeks, gently rubbing the hot, red flesh. There was, indeed, plenty of time for some makeup sex before she drifted off into a sound, dreamless sleep.

The next day, GG felt like a different person. She was organized and efficient, her work going smoothly; by lunchtime, the shop was really starting to look the way she wanted it to. Her bottom was a little tender, but most of the effects of her spanking were gone and she paid attention to the time so she could stop for lunch. She took a real break over her sandwich and her bowl of fresh fruit, reading a new book while she ate and sipped a bottle of water. She was so pleased at the end of the day that she twirled in a little spin of pleasure at the way the shop was coming together. She started to walk out and ran smack into her husband.

"Leo! Oh, I'm so glad you're here! Come in, come in." She grabbed his hand and pulled him in after her.

"Wow!" Leo exclaimed. "Look at this place! It doesn't even look like the same place I walked into yesterday."

"I know!" GG hugged herself in excited glee. "I got so much done and everything just fell into place like it was all planned for years."

Leo grinned at her. "I bet you ate lunch too, didn't you?"

She narrowed her eyes but grinned at him. "Not only that, but I also sat down and read my new book while I ate and took my time."

He put his arms around her and hugged her hard, lifting her chin so he could kiss her.

"Thank you for everything," GG murmured.

"Are you actually thanking me for a spanking?" Leo teased.

"Well, I wouldn't quite say that, but… I guess, sort of."

He kissed her again and said, "I love you, GG. I just want you safe and healthy."

The next couple of weeks went smoothly and GG had the shop all arranged the way she wanted it three weeks before her grand opening date. The baker in the space next door was on schedule to open the same weekend and she would be serving bite-sized samples of her work with tiny cups of coffee or punch. Her name was Izzy and she was a bit of an aging hippy, but she had a talent for baking and GG hoped she would be successful. She had ambitions of eventually turning her bakery into a sort of cafe, where she could serve lunch, but she wasn't at that stage yet. She named her place The Lovin' Oven and it was an eclectic mix of styles that Izzy had somehow managed to make work together.

By the time the grand opening arrived, GG had gone over everything what seemed like a million times. She was as ready as it was possible to be. The first customer walked in exactly ten seconds after she turned her sign to *Open* and there was a steady stream of people for the first three hours. Izzy was busy too, as far as GG could see, and when there was finally a little lull, GG opened a cold bottle of water with a relieved sigh. She had already sold twice as much as she ever had in a days' time in her smaller shop and she couldn't get the smile off her face. Izzy dashed over with a little plate of treats for her and she was nearly dancing with excitement at the way the morning was going. GG had been sure to bring a couple of sandwiches with her, just so she could snatch a bite here and there when she had time.

Early in the afternoon, Leo walked in, followed by four ladies who were wives of men who worked at Leo's firm. Leo had made sure that their husbands had let them know about GG's grand opening and they had decided to visit the shop and then make it an afternoon by going out for lunch and drinks afterward. GG hugged her husband and whispered her thanks for his thoughtfulness and went to help the four women, who all spent their money freely. GG was beaming as they left nearly an hour later and Leo winked at her.

"Their husbands all said they love to shop," he said with a chuckle.

"Boy, they sure did. I'd be glad to have them back anytime!"

"It looks like you've sold half your inventory," Leo said, looking around the shop.

"It's been really good," answered GG with a proud grin.

Next, Katie and her daughter-in-law walked through the

door, followed by Sharon, and there were excited squeals and hugs all around. Leo kissed his wife and ducked out the door to check out the bakery before he headed home. The three women bought several things each and by the time they were finished, it was close enough to closing time that GG opened the bottle of champagne she had chilling and they all toasted the new shop. The day was even more than GG had hoped it would be and she sighed happily as she locked up and left for the day. Leo was waiting with another chilled bottle of champagne and a plate of shrimp cocktail, along with a tray of crab-stuffed mushrooms and a tray of chunks of tender steak wrapped in flaky pastry crusts, ready to pop into the oven.

GG melted into his kiss and then looked at the treats he had arranged. "What did you do?" she asked in awe.

"I got a recommendation for a place that makes party trays to go and I ordered some."

"How far did you have to go? There's no place like that around here."

Leo laughed. "I had to travel a little, but it was worth it. Look what you did today!"

She wound herself around him again and said, "I love you so much." The kiss they shared was fiery.

"I should put these in the oven," Leo said.

"Will it hurt if you put them in the fridge for a while first?" GG asked.

"No, that's what you do until you're ready for them."

"Then I think we should postpone the food until after the appetizer," GG said, gliding up and down against him.

Leo lost his breath and captured her mouth with his. "I think that's a great idea."

GG locked the door and the two of them chased each other up the stairs.

Chapter 6

GG was extra busy for a couple of weeks after her grand opening, contacting her artists and ordering new stock, unpacking and staging new pieces, meeting with several artists who wanted to see the shop and show her their work. She made phone calls to each person who had pieces to sell on opening day, and that was most of them. She placed a small ad in the trail rider's magazine, knowing that riding season was just around the corner and that a lot of the people who came to camp and ride in the park would ride into town. There were hitching posts all along Main Street to accommodate them and a water trough was kept filled with clean, fresh water at one end of the street.

GG had just walked in the door at the end of the day; Leo had beaten her home and had already changed out of his business clothes. They went through their usual after-work routine of discussing how their days had gone over a beer for Leo and a glass of wine for GG. She was giggling as she told him about a lady who had come into the shop looking for one very specific item and ended up going home with two bags of gifts and a painting. The phone rang and Leo picked it up. He had trouble hearing the person on the other end, and as GG watched, his face went pale with shock. He asked a couple of questions and wrote something down and then he hung up, taking a deep breath before he turned to GG.

She was staring at him with dread. He looked the way he did when he had gotten the news that his father had passed away. "Leo… what is it? What happened?"

Slowly, he said, "That was a woman named Margaret Chase. She was calling from Africa. It's Bryce."

GG went white as a sheet. "Oh, no… no! Is he alive?"

Leo reached for her as he numbly shook his head. "It was an accident… they were riding in a rocky place out along a riverbank and they hit a big hole. Bryce was thrown out of the vehicle and hit his head on a rock. He was killed instantly."

GG let out a howl of grief and shock and Leo pulled her close to him, trying to offer what solace he could and knowing that he couldn't comfort her. She doubled over in pain, weeping like a child, and tears streamed down Leo's face as he held her. It was a long time before she regained a little bit of control.

"Oh, my God. Mom and Dad… and Carl, they're twins. How can this be happening? He was done with the dangerous work. Oh, God, Leo, this isn't fair!" She broke down again.

A few minutes later, GG's father called. Margot had taken a sedative and cried herself to sleep and Don wept with his daughter and then hung up so he could call Carl. The whole family was devastated, but maybe Carl more than anyone. Carl and Bryce had always had that particularly close bond that twins had; they'd always been on the same wavelength, each understanding the other without words. It was like having half of his own life ripped away. GG spoke to him a little later and then she sank to the floor in a flood of grief. Leo gathered her up and carried her to the couch, where he held her in his lap, and she cried until she had no tears left then slept the sleep of emotional exhaustion, cradled against his shoulder.

It was a nightmare to get Bryce's body shipped home, but Don handled it. He spoke to Margaret several times and he heard the love and grief in her voice when she talked about his son. She promised to pack up his personal belongings and send them to GG and Leo's address. She would be staying on in Africa to carry on the work she had been doing with Bryce. When the package arrived with Bryce's belongings, it included an envelope full of cards that the children had made, expressing their love for Bryce and their sadness at his death. Leo had asked GG to wait until he was with her to open the large boxes and they went through them together.

GG found a shoebox full of letters she had written to her brother throughout his career and his years away from home. There was another one full of letters from their parents and yet another one from Carl. Bryce had saved every one of them and it was easy to see that he'd read them over and over. There were photos and other mementos and some folders full of articles he'd written and published in magazines and newspapers. There was a knife that he had carried in a sheath on his hip and GG set that aside for Carl. There was a worn Bible that had gone everywhere with him. There were also a few pictures of Bryce in Africa, posing with the children and more with a woman dressed in khaki shorts and shirt, with sturdy boots and her dark hair tied back. In one picture, the two of them had their arms around each other's waists and carefree grins on their faces. Bryce and Margaret, 2000 was written on the back of the picture.

"Look, Leo, this is Margaret." Quiet tears trickled down GG's face as she looked at it. "They look so happy together." She just couldn't get over the shock of her brother's sudden death.

"They do," Leo said. "She must be a very special woman.

All these letters he saved… family meant everything to him, didn't it?"

"Yes. I just can't believe he's gone."

The funeral was an ordeal that tested the whole family. It was a shock to them to see the people who turned out to pay their respects to Bryce. It was national news and cards and letters arrived from around the whole country and several other countries. He had made a mark in the world of journalism, and he had become an easily recognized face on national news programs. There was an outpouring of sympathy that touched his family and was also a little overwhelming.

When the ceremonies were finally over and Bryce had been laid to rest in the family plot next to Quyen, the family was exhausted. GG was just thankful that the story of Bryce and his brief marriage had been kept private, or it would have been spread all over the news. It was just too personal to have it turn into a public story. GG kept all the news clippings and articles, two copies of each so that she could send one to Margaret. She had called on the day of the funeral and let them know that the school she and Bryce had been working on was being named the Bryce Devereaux Children's School. It meant a great deal to them all and Margaret promised to send them pictures once the school was complete and the sign was put in place.

A few days after Bryce's funeral, his parents left for Florida. They were going to stop and see Leo's mother and Margot told GG that they felt the need for hot sun, sandy beaches, and healing sea breezes. Their goodbyes were sweet but sad and GG and Leo stood waving until they were out of sight. Carl and Peggy had come to say goodbye and they left soon after Don and Margot did. Carl looked like he had aged ten years since his brother's death and GG hugged his wife, Peggy, and whispered to her to take care of him. Peggy hugged her back hard and promised.

Shelby sat there with tears flowing down her cheeks and said, "Oh, Gran, that's so sad. He finally gave up all his dangerous assignments and then a stupid accident took him? It's so unfair."

GG's eyes were shiny with tears. "It was unfair and it was such a shock. It took a long, long time for the pain to heal a little bit."

"What happened to Margaret?"

"She stayed on in Africa for years, carrying on her work. She sent the pictures of the school and it's still named the Bryce Devereaux Children's School to this day. Eventually, she met a surgeon from the Mercy Ship that performs surgeries there every year and they fell in love and got married. We still exchange Christmas cards every year."

"That's so sweet."

"How are you feeling? I think we should have a break, don't you? I've got a bowl of chicken salad and some fresh croissants in the kitchen."

"That sounds wonderful. Maggie's croissants?"

"I wouldn't have any other, would you?'

Shelby laughed and struggled to her feet, rubbing the small of her back with a groan.

"Are you okay?"

"I am; my back seems to ache all the time these days. Let's have some lunch and I'll stretch a little."

"Excellent idea."

GG went through the days as if she was operating on autopilot, taking care of her responsibilities, but feeling slightly numb all the time. She had lost her cheerful, upbeat outlook and her energy; she felt tired constantly. Leo tried everything he could think of to comfort her and help her feel better, but nothing seemed to work. She found it impossible to accept the fact that her brother had been taken so suddenly. It continued to shock her every time she thought about it and even though she knew that life had to go on, she just couldn't find a way to accept it. Leo watched her withdraw further and further each day, it seemed, and he just couldn't find a way to reach her. She did the things she was supposed to do and she gave all the right answers when people talked to her, but her spark was gone.

Leo and GG sat at the dinner table, mostly in silence. Leo watched his wife pick at her food and asked, "How was your day? Was the shop busy?"

"It was fine. Kind of slow." She didn't ask how his day had been.

Leo tried again. "I've got an idea. Why don't we pack up the camper and go see your parents for a few days? They're not that far from here right now, right?"

GG looked up, startled. "No, but I can't do that right now. I have things going on at the shop. It's not a very good time to take off."

"It would do us good, GG. And your parents would love it."

"Leo, I just don't feel up to that. It's a lot of work getting the camper ready to go, cleaning and packing and remembering everything that we need to take with us. Then, when we get back, there's even more work unpacking it and cleaning again. No, I just can't do it right now."

"Come on, baby, I can help you with all that. Let's just say the hell with everything and go."

"You're not listening to me. I don't feel up to it."

"Then let's get the girls for a few days, Carter too if he doesn't have any sports going on."

GG looked exasperated. "Why can't you listen to me? I don't feel up to it."

Leo was honestly shocked that she was turning down the idea of having her grandbabies to visit. He studied her for a few moments and then said carefully, "I think you should go see Doc Harper. Go get a physical, see if there's something wrong. You shouldn't be this tired all the time. You've never passed up an opportunity to spend time with your grandchildren."

"There's nothing wrong with me!" GG snapped. "I just need time, that's all."

"GG, a lot of time has passed but you're still not yourself. I know grief is hard and it has its own timetable, but I think you need some help. I'm obviously not helping you, so maybe someone else could."

"What exactly are you getting at? You think I need some kind of… of counseling or something? You think I'm crazy?"

"Of course not! But you've had a shocking and terrible loss and it wouldn't be a bit unusual to become depressed because of it."

GG's face was flushed. "I am not depressed! I'm grieving; that's not depression. Like I said, I just need some time."

Leo reached for her hand but she jerked it away. "I feel like you're out of my reach. Let me help you, let me comfort you, GG."

There was a quick sheen of tears in her eyes and she said desperately, "You can't help me, Leo. I have to get through this my way. I'm doing the best I can and I honestly feel like I just need time to heal."

His heart sank and he said helplessly, "All right. I can't tell you how to grieve, I know that. It just hurts to see you like this. I want to do something to make it better. I need you back, baby."

"Please, Leo, I can't take care of you now; it's all I can do to take care of myself. Please, just let me do it."

He took her hand even though she tried to pull it away. "I'll give you time, GG, but I'm not letting you slip too far away. Pay attention when I tell you that I won't let that happen."

There was a little flash of rebellion in her eyes, but she didn't say anything. Over the next few days, GG was a bit more talkative with Leo, but it was obvious to him that she was forcing herself to do it. All the same, he figured it was a step in the right direction so he accepted it as a positive sign. Nearly every night she went to bed early, so that she was asleep by the time he joined her in bed. He tried going to bed at the same time she did, hoping he could get her to talk to him or get her to cuddle in his arms, but she stiffened when he tried and drew away from him as quickly as she could.

One of the senior engineers at Leo's firm retired unexpectedly and left them shorthanded during a particularly busy time. Leo found himself working late, even working on some Saturdays. It kept him busy and left him with less time to fret over GG's continued distance from him. She wasn't really interested in hearing his work stories and didn't tell him much about her own, so he immersed himself in work and let her have the time she had asked for. Even after an engineer was hired, she was a junior engineer and had a lot to learn, so the workload didn't change much. Several weeks went by that way and it began to seem that it was normal, at least to GG. Leo still missed her and their old closeness, but he thought he was doing what she needed by giving her time and space.

GG's work life was busy too; she was actively looking for new artists, especially since she had lost three in recent days. One had retired, one had moved away, and the other had a new baby and was taking a long break from her artistry. GG needed to bring some new things into the shop and she began to be interested in a couple of people she had heard of who were a little farther away. She thought it over carefully and decided that it would be worth it to travel to meet them and discuss their work. Once she made up her mind to do it, she knew she was going to have to convince Leo that it was a good idea. She went home and made his favorite meatloaf dinner and waited for him to get home.

Dusk was falling and GG had long since turned off the oven, and Leo still wasn't home from work. She realized, as her irritation grew, that he'd been having a lot of late nights. She decided that she was going to take her business trip and if her husband didn't like it, that was just too bad. "He's not even home most of the time, anyway, why should he care if I'm gone for a couple of days?" she muttered to herself. She poured herself a second glass of wine and was sitting at the kitchen table when he finally came in.

"Wow, something smells good," Leo said with a grin, hoping that his wife was finally making a turn for the better.

"I don't know why," she answered shortly. "If I hadn't turned it off a long time ago, it would have been burned to a crisp."

He bent to kiss her and she turned her head so that his kiss landed on her cheek. "Sorry, it's just been so crazy at work, it's hard to get out of there. If I'd known you were doing this, I'd have left it for tomorrow."

"I'll warm it up," GG said stiffly and went to put his plate in the microwave.

"Have you eaten?" Leo asked.

"Yes, I ate before it got cold." She set his plate on the table and he got himself a beer.

GG sipped her wine while Leo ate, clearly enjoying the meal and thanking her several times. She listened to him talk about his job for a little while and then finally said, "I've been busy at the shop too. In fact, I need to talk to you about that."

"Sure, what's up?" He was thrilled that she actually wanted to talk to him about her shop.

"I've lost three of my artists and my stock is low. There are a couple of people I've been interested in talking to; one is a sculptor and my pottery expert is moving to Georgia. They're both in the St. Louis area and I need to take a couple of days to go see them."

"Oh," Leo said, not sure what to think of what she'd said. "I don't think there's any way that I can take time off work right now."

"No, obviously you're too busy for that. I'll go myself. I'm perfectly capable of driving to St. Louis and meeting with them. I should be able to see them both in one day, so I'll only be gone overnight. It's no big deal, but I really need to do it."

Leo was silent for a moment, thinking it over. He finally thought that if this was what it took to get her interested in things again, it would be worth it. "Are you sure you want to do this by yourself?"

"Well, it would be easier if we could both go, but it'll be fine. And maybe it would be good for me to expand a little. I'm a business owner, I shouldn't be limited to only the artists who are right in our neck of the woods."

He had a sinking feeling that nothing was better, but he resolutely pushed it away. It had to be good for GG to be more active and more involved, surely it would lead to good things. She had to get interested in life again in order to be herself and maybe work was the thing that would get her interested. He decided that he would give her his support and hope for the best. He just desperately wanted to see her get her enthusiasm back; if this didn't work, he would have to find another way to get through to her.

"When are you going to go?" he asked casually, as if it was something that happened all the time.

GG was surprised that he agreed so easily, but she hid it

and answered just as casually. "I'm not sure yet. I'm waiting for the sculptor to get back to me and then I'll call the other woman and see if I can see her the following morning. She makes all kinds of gorgeous things out of stained glass; I'd love to see her work in my shop."

So Leo hid his misgivings and concentrated on the fact that she actually *had* sounded enthusiastic about the new artists. Hopefully this would be the turning point that she needed. Once she got the appointments set up, he changed the oil in her car and insisted on putting new tires on for her.

"You probably have some more miles to go on this set, but I'd feel better if you take this trip on new ones," Leo said.

"All right, I don't really think it's necessary, but thank you," GG said.

He carried her bag to the car for her early in the morning when she was ready to go and she turned her face up for a kiss, giving him renewed hope that this trip was a good thing. He watched her back out of the driveway and waved as she pulled away, standing and watching until her car was out of sight. Then he sighed and said out loud, "I sure hope this isn't a mistake."

Chapter 7

GG had an excellent meeting with the sculptor in the afternoon and left with a signed contract and several pieces to put in the shop right away. She had a reservation in a nice hotel in a safe area and she checked in and enjoyed the feeling of having a new artist whose pieces she could sell. She stretched out on the bed and rested for a bit and realized with a pang that she missed being able to tell Leo all about it. Then the thought of Bryce crossed her mind and she felt the familiar stab of grief and immediately felt guilty for enjoying the accomplishment she'd made. How could she feel like celebrating when Bryce's life was over? The weight of his loss passed over her again, like a crushing weight, and her good feelings were swept away in a flash.

GG took a little nap and woke to realize that she was hungry and it was time to get some dinner. She freshened up a little and went down to the hotel restaurant. She had chosen the hotel partly because it had a restaurant that had a reputation for excellent food and she wouldn't have to venture out again to get her dinner. The place lived up to its reputation and she had a delicious meal and a glass of wine in a pleasant atmosphere. There was a nice-looking man about Leo's age sitting at the bar and she glanced up twice to catch him looking at her. She averted her eyes quickly but the waitress came over to tell her that he was offering to buy her another glass of wine.

Alarmed, GG said, "No! Please, tell him thanks but absolutely not."

The waitress was quick to reassure her. "I'll tell him. Don't worry, he's a regular here and he wouldn't dream of being pushy."

"Good," GG said and then blushed a deep red when the waitress spoke to the man and he turned and gave GG a wink. She was finished with her dinner, and she signed for it, then returned to her room, locking the door securely. She felt suddenly lonely and picked up the phone to call Leo. There was no answer and she looked at the clock; it was after seven and she wondered where he was. Probably working late again, or maybe he stopped on his way home for dinner.

"Good lord, GG, you're not eighteen years old anymore. You ought to be able to spend a night away from home without missing your husband, for heaven's sake. It's only one night; you should have done this a long time ago. You're a grown woman!" But then the thought crossed her mind that she could count on one hand the number of nights she and Leo had spent apart. Grown woman or not, overwhelmed with grief or not, she missed her husband. Maybe this experience was going to be good for them somehow. She thought about the man at the bar and her reaction to him, and she missed Leo even more. Well, she would be back home tomorrow, and maybe she'd just tell him how much she had missed him. The thought made her smile a little.

GG had another successful meeting with the stained-glass artist and she was happy to acknowledge that her little trip had been a big success. She had a quick lunch before she left St.

Louis and then started for home. She felt lighter than she had when she had started the trip and she thought that it must have been good for her. She even found herself smiling a few times when she thought about the success of her trip. Maybe the next time, she and Leo would be able to go together. That made her smile too. She even sang along with the radio a few times during her drive.

It was a little after five when GG pulled into the garage, feeling quietly happy to be back home. Leo wasn't home yet, but it was early and she went inside and unpacked, tossing clothes into the hamper and putting her toiletry items away. She brought the boxes from the artists in too, planning to show the pieces to Leo. At six, he still wasn't home and she poured herself a glass of wine and waited. At almost seven, she heard the garage door open and just a minute later, her husband came through the door, wearing a cautious smile. GG smiled back at him and he crossed the room quickly and pulled her into his arms for a kiss.

"I'm sorry, I wanted to get home earlier but I just couldn't get away. How did it go?"

GG said, "It went well, I got contracts with both artists and a box full of pieces from both of them too."

"That's great!" Leo looked impressed. "Have you been here long?"

"I got here a little after five. I've already unpacked."

"Damn, I'm really sorry. I wanted to be here to meet you."

GG said, "It's nothing to worry about, I know work has been crazy."

"It had better let up soon, these late nights are getting old. Can I see what you brought back? Are you hungry?" Leo felt a little bit like a kid on Christmas morning.

"I am, how about you?"

"I am too. Do you want to go out?"

GG said, "No, it's been a long day. I'll just make some sandwiches, is that okay with you?"

Leo said, "Sandwiches would be perfect." He didn't know what had happened, but he felt a whole new vibe coming from his wife that he hadn't felt since before Bryce had died. He said a silent prayer of thanks and went to change his clothes. "Give me a minute to change and I'll help you with the sandwiches."

The two of them made turkey and cheese sandwiches with all the fixings and Leo opened a bag of potato chips. After they ate, GG showed her new treasures to Leo and he was honestly impressed with the quality of the work she'd brought back.

"These should be popular," Leo said. "That stained glass hanging would look great in the kitchen window, wouldn't it?"

"It really would," said GG, "and it would send color all over the kitchen when the sun shines through that window."

"And these bowls. Are they suitable for serving food?"

GG nodded. "They are. They'd make great serving dishes, wouldn't they? And this one has four small bowls that go with it. They're great salad or dessert bowls."

The two of them talked while they ate their sandwiches, more conversation than they had shared in weeks. For the first time in weeks, GG didn't excuse herself to go to bed early and it seemed like old times as they took turns in their bathroom, brushing their teeth and getting ready for bed. They got into bed together and Leo switched off the lamp and slipped his arm under GG's shoulders. He didn't make another move, content to lie there, relaxed and comfortable. GG stiffened slightly before she gave a little sigh and relaxed. The day caught up with her and when she yawned, Leo chuckled and gave her a little squeeze.

"Good night, baby," he said softly and the two of them

had the most restful night together that they'd had in a long time.

GG was busy in her shop, staging her new items and rearranging the not-so-new ones. She greeted a couple of customers and helped one of them try to decide between two of the new stained-glass hangings. She was feeling a little better than she had before her trip to St. Louis, as if she was slowly emerging from the fog of grief that had been choking her. She and Leo were still feeling their way back to each other, a little at a time, largely because Leo didn't want to push her. She still had her low points, but she was definitely improving. Leo had promised to try to be home by six and she was going to make his meatloaf dinner again.

GG was finishing up and getting ready to close at her usual Wednesday time of three p.m. and the shop was already empty of customers. She had to stop at Vance's to get a few things for dinner and she slipped out a few minutes early and locked up. She was looking over the peaches at the little grocery store when she heard a couple of women talking nearby.

"So what does Greg think of the latest engineer?"

"Well, obviously, she's younger than everyone else and she's single and pretty, so I guess he thinks what they all do."

The first woman said, "It's just weird, isn't it? The whole firm has never had a female engineer before. It must be odd."

"It just seems weird to me because they really needed an experienced engineer and she's just a junior and has so much to learn before she can be a lot of help. Jefferson was a senior engineer when he retired, so I don't understand why they didn't hire someone who was experienced."

"Well, I guess women are getting hired everywhere these days, aren't they?"

"Yeah. As long as it's not *my* husband who has to work all the extra hours training her, I don't mind."

"You and me both!"

The other women moved on and GG stood there, unable to move. It was obviously Leo's firm that they had been talking about. He had never once mentioned that their new engineer was a woman. He'd been working late nights and Saturdays for weeks to train a *woman* without ever seeing fit to mention it to his wife. It made GG feel ill to think of why he hadn't ever told her. She mechanically bought what she needed and then drove home. Her head was swimming with confused thoughts about what she'd heard. She remembered when the man had tried to buy her a drink in the hotel restaurant and how quickly it had made her uneasy, even alarmed. Then she thought about Leo and that he could never be capable of that kind of betrayal.

GG put her groceries away and mixed up her meatloaf, still thinking in confused circles. She thought again that Leo, her Leo, could never be unfaithful. Then she wanted to kick herself for even having such a thought in connection with Leo. But the thoughts of the past few months crept into her head and she knew how she had pushed him away, refusing to touch him or even speak to him. It had literally been months since she and her husband had been intimate with each other and she was struck with self-recrimination for the way she had turned away from him. The thought went through her mind; who could blame him for straying? Then she was immediately angry. She'd been grieving, she'd been incapacitated by her loss, that was no excuse for her husband to take his comfort with another woman.

GG's head was pounding as she put the meatloaf in the oven. She didn't know what to think; she had never in her life been so confused. She thought of how many hours Leo had spent at "work" that he had never spent before. And he hadn't ever told her about the new engineer. Of course, she hadn't really been speaking to him at all for most of that time. But that was beside the point. Something this important, he should have told her, even if he had to make her listen. Now it seemed that he'd been hiding it from her. She refused to see the fact that hiding it was kind of impossible in a small-town life like they had in Boone, Indiana. It was bound to come out. Unless... unless he thought that she was such a trusting, foolish soul that she would never believe such a thing about her husband. Face it, she'd been such a small-town girl that when a man offered to buy her a drink, she'd nearly been struck by panic. Maybe she really was that trusting and foolish.

She had to get herself together; she only had an hour before Leo would be home and she had to figure out how she was going to handle this. The potatoes and meatloaf were in the oven and the peach crisp was done. She went into the bathroom and splashed cool water on her face and then she went back to the kitchen and got herself some aspirin. She had no desire to accuse Leo of something when all she had was speculation and suspicion. She had to find out something real first; it would be too awful on her part to accuse him if it wasn't true. She needed to know. She took a deep breath and told herself that she had to set it aside somehow, shut it off in the back of her mind and keep it there until she actually found out something factual. She couldn't let Leo know that she had these suspicions.

When Leo got home, he walked into the house and greeted GG with a real smile; it was obvious how happy he was to see her. He put his arms around her and kissed her with all the tenderness that he'd shown her countless times before.

"Oh, Lord, GG, it smells great in here. Are you making what I think you are?"

She smiled at him. "I'm making your favorites. And you made it home right on time."

"It's gotten really old, working all these hours. I hope it's easing up. I told them it was time for me to go back to regular hours. If they keep sticking me with the extra work, I'll put my foot down. I've done my share." He gave her another kiss and accepted the cold beer she handed to him. "I'm going to change my clothes, I'll be right back."

Somehow GG got through dinner with Leo without breaking down and betraying the ugly thoughts she'd been having. By the time they finished, she could almost believe that she'd dreamed it all. Everything seemed so normal; how could her husband possibly be cheating on her? It wasn't in him to do a thing like that. She needed to forget it; it was impossible. When they finished dinner, Leo helped her put the dirty dishes in the dishwasher and wipe down the table and countertops. Then he took her hand and led her to the couch to watch a little TV with him. He put his arm around her and gently drew her close to him, and after a while, he turned her face to his and kissed her, gently at first and then a little deeper. GG had a moment of utter panic and confusion and then she forced her doubts away and let herself sink into the kiss. It was so familiar, how could it ever be wrong?

Leo gathered his wife up and settled her into his lap, cradling her in his arms. He kissed her, exploring her mouth gently but deeply, twining his fingers in her hair and leaving her mouth to kiss her eyelids, light as a feather. He trailed little butterfly kisses down her cheek and her throat, trailing his fingertips down to the swell of her breasts and stroking her soft skin with a sigh of pure pleasure. He spent eternity unbuttoning her blouse, one button at a time, revealing an inch or two of creamy skin with each one, stroking and kissing. GG writhed on his lap, his touch sending little shivers of sensation down her spine and making her moan just a little bit in the back of her throat. Leo slipped her blouse down over her shoulders and off, kissing her shoulder and nibbling at her collarbone. GG shivered in helpless delight at the sensations that prickled her skin.

When Leo reached behind her to unfasten her bra, she let her head drop back and closed her eyes as his warm hand cupped her bare breast, gently rubbing his thumb back and forth over the rosy peak, causing her gasp of pleasure. He fondled her breasts, squeezing them and gently pulling at her swollen nipples until she cried out in a wordless plea for more. He leaned her back until she rested against the arm of the couch and then, finally, his mouth found her firm mounds, kissing, licking, suckling the swollen tips until she cried out again. She was lost in sensation, well, almost lost, but when he stroked her thigh, bringing his hand up under her skirt, she suddenly stiffened in instinctive protest. His hand stilled and then gently went on up until he reached the vee between her legs.

In a panic, GG burst into tears, struggling to get away from him. Leo was completely shocked, trying to soothe her without having any idea what was wrong. GG broke down into deep, wracking sobs and Leo put his arms around her and rocked her, crooning to her and trying to calm her. She wept until there were no more tears and she was limp with sheer exhaustion. Leo picked her up and carried her to the bedroom, where he settled her gently into their bed and covered her. He kissed her forehead and walked away, leaving her in peace. He went to the kitchen and poured a stiff drink of whiskey. When he finally went to bed, he kissed her forehead again and whispered to her, "It's all right, baby, it's just a little too soon. I love you, we'll figure it out." It was late when he finally drifted into a restless sleep.

Chapter 8

The next days were the most difficult days Leo had ever had with GG. She refused to talk about what had happened between them. She refused to talk about her feelings, she refused to talk about Bryce; in fact, she refused to talk about pretty much anything. She was moody and temperamental, sometimes silent and sullen, and other times ready to fly into a rage at the slightest provocation. Leo was at his wit's end; he tried every way he could think of to get through to her and nothing worked. He thought about going to Katie to ask her opinion, but he knew she was busy with her job and her new grandbaby, so he just couldn't bring himself to burden her with his problems.

GG drove to where Leo worked, to get a glimpse of the woman she suspected he was spending all his time with, and she felt as if she'd been stabbed in the heart when she saw how young and attractive she was. No wonder Leo was never home. The jealousy ate at her, even though she never saw an improper move between them. She watched, taking a well-hidden table in a restaurant near the firm where Leo and his apprentice went for lunch. Again, she saw nothing improper, but the two of them had an easy camaraderie and were clearly comfortable together. After she left the restaurant, GG drove back to Boone but she had to pull off the road when she burst into tears, the image of her husband and the pretty young woman burned into her brain.

GG stewed over the situation for a couple of days, knowing that she had to do something; life couldn't go on like it was and she had a real urge to strike back at Leo for his betrayal. So she planned what seemed like a fitting revenge for what she was sure was her husband's unfaithfulness. She cooked a delicious meal and chilled a bottle of wine and when Leo got home from work, she was dressed in a low-cut sweater that accentuated her cleavage and a tight little skirt that she'd never worn anywhere but in the house to tempt her husband. When Leo walked into the house, his eyes widened in shock at the sight of her, bustling around the kitchen. He approached her cautiously and she turned and gave him a smile.

"Good, you're home early," GG said lightly as he gave her a kiss on the cheek. "I wanted to make a special dinner."

"What's the occasion?" Leo asked, accepting the beer she handed to him.

"It's just been too long since we had a special dinner together, don't you think?"

"It's been a long time." He bent his head and caught her lips with his, the kiss gently probing, lingering for a bit. GG didn't pull away and he dared to hope that she was starting to open up to him.

"How was your day?" GG asked as she stirred something in a pot on the stove.

"It was good. We're making good progress on the Court Street bridge project. How was yours?"

"Oh, the usual. I'm sure you'd find it boring. I'm just a shopkeeper in a small town. That's nothing like an engineer designing important projects that affect thousands of people."

Leo looked at her strangely. "GG, I thought you loved your shop. You've made a real success out of it."

She waved a hand. "I do love it; it's just not on a scale with the kind of work you do. But then, I'd never have made it through something like engineering school." She laughed lightly.

Leo said, "Well, engineering is not your kind of thing. I spend all day with blueprints and plans and you spend your days with people. I could never make a success of the kind of thing you're good at. You have a way with people. It's special."

"Our appetizers will be ready in a couple of minutes. Do you want to change clothes?"

"Yeah, I do, I'll be right back."

When he came back, she had poured herself a glass of wine and put it on the coffee table in front of the couch facing the fireplace and set a fresh beer there too. She was just carrying in a tray of stuffed mushrooms and some little plates and they sat down together in front of the fire to enjoy the appetizers. Leo didn't know what had come over her, but he was thrilled with the change. They chatted about Carter's little league and the fact that the girls would be starting kindergarten in the fall. GG talked about how cute Katie's new grandson was and how the little baby had his daddy wrapped around his little finger already. When GG made a move to return to the kitchen, Leo caught her hand and drew her against him for another kiss. She melted against him as his kiss deepened and he explored her mouth with his tongue until she finally drew her head away.

"I don't want to burn dinner," GG murmured huskily. "Food first."

Leo watched her go, his heart lighter than it had been for weeks. He was smiling when he joined her in the kitchen. They enjoyed their dinner and talked more than they had in what seemed like forever. GG drank another glass of wine and flirted a little with her husband. He enjoyed every second of it, feeling like his wife had come back to him. After dinner, they cleaned up the mess together and then they went back to the couch in the den. Leo put his arm around GG and she laid her head on his shoulder, gazing into the fire. After a few minutes, Leo put his finger under her chin and tipped her head up to meet his kiss. GG drew away and got to her feet.

"I'm going to go up and change," she said softly.

Leo gave her a wink and said, "I'll put out the fire and lock up."

He watched her walk away and then turned off the gas log and locked the house up for the night. When he got to the bedroom, GG was dressed in a filmy little gown that left little to the imagination and Leo's mouth suddenly went dry. He crossed the room in a few long strides and wrapped her in his arms, his mouth finding hers. He kissed her until she gasped for breath and he cupped her breasts, the firm peaks jutting into his palms through the flimsy fabric of her gown. She could feel his erection jutting against her belly and when he groaned, she suddenly stiffened and pulled away from him.

"Your things are in the guest room," she said, her voice hard and brittle.

Swept by shock, he said, "The guest room… what are you talking about?"

"That's where you're sleeping tonight, Leo. I'm sleeping by myself. You honestly think that I'd ignore everything and fall into bed with you just like everything is normal? You don't deserve it. Now get out." She gave him a push toward the door and pointed to the hallway.

Leo was overwhelmed with anger and he shouted, "What the hell is *wrong* with you? You did all this on purpose tonight, didn't you?"

"What's wrong with me? What's wrong with you? You think you can behave the way you have and then just take me to bed like everything is fine?" She was shouting right back at him.

"Behave what way? I don't have a clue what you're talking about! Have you lost your mind?" He had never been so angry in his life.

"Oh, you think about it a little bit, Leo. I'm sure you can figure it out. Now get out!"

Leo fought to restrain himself, and after staring at her for another second, he turned and stalked out of the room without another word. He heard the door slam behind him and the lock turn and he stood there, breathing hard. He had a strong urge to toss her over his knee and spank some sense into her, but he was entirely too angry to do it right then. He went down to the kitchen and poured a whiskey, tossing it back and muttering to himself. He poured another whiskey and sipped it this time, thinking over the whole evening in growing bewilderment. He didn't have any idea what had set her off or what she had to be so angry about. He had no clue what was going on in her head, but it was time to find out and it was time to put an end to it.

When GG emerged from the bedroom the next morning, Leo was already gone. She had tossed and turned all night, unable to sleep until an hour or so before dawn. She kept picturing Leo's face when she had told him to get out and she was increasingly uneasy about it. He had seemed to be so completely shocked and he honestly didn't seem to have any idea what she was angry about. Could she possibly be completely wrong about the whole thing? No, there were too many things that pointed right to the conclusion she'd come to. All the late nights, the Saturdays when he was supposed to be working. The pretty young woman, obviously perfectly comfortable with *her* husband. The fact that she and Leo hadn't made love for months and he was so patient and understanding about it. What kind of man acted like that? That thought increased her uneasiness. Leo was the most understanding man in the world, especially with her. But then she pictured him in the restaurant with the other woman and she shook her head violently. No, there was no way she could be wrong about it. It was just… Leo had always been the perfect husband and it was so hard to accept that he could do this to her.

He had made a pot of coffee and it was still hot, so she poured herself a cup. Suddenly she realized that she had no idea what she should do next. She hadn't thought past the plan she had carried out last night and that was all about hurting him back. Now what? What did women do when this kind of thing happened to them? They forgave their husbands and tried to find a way to live with the betrayal, or they got divorced. The idea of divorcing Leo left a hollow pain in the pit of her stomach. She couldn't even imagine it. But how did she just live with what he'd done? And what if *he* didn't want to stay married? That thought had never even occurred to her. What if she'd just given him a reason to walk away? That was the worst thought she'd ever had and she realized she was about to break down in tears yet again.

"God, GG, you've got to get hold of yourself," she said out loud. "This is a nightmare." She decided to go up and take a long, hot shower. Maybe it would clear her head a little. And then she'd go to work; maybe if she stayed busy, she could think of something sensible to do.

It was Friday and when GG got home, Leo wasn't there yet. She stood in the kitchen trying to decide what to do; making dinner as usual seemed crazily inappropriate, but she didn't know what else to do. She finally settled for making a pot of chicken noodle soup and then she basically paced the kitchen until Leo finally got home.

He didn't speak to her when he came in until after he'd hung up his coat and changed his clothes. Then he came into the kitchen and looked directly at her. "I've got to go out of town tomorrow. I'm leaving in the morning and I'll be home on Sunday. When I get home, we're going to talk. Now I'm going up to pack a bag and then I'm going to the Burger Barn for dinner. You'll have the house to yourself. I'll sleep in the guest room again, so you won't be bothered." With that, he went back upstairs to pack his things.

GG was stunned into silence. She began to feel that she had made a dreadful mistake, and if she had, she didn't know how she could ever make it right. Leo came back down and left without saying anything else to her. GG sank into the corner of the couch and tried to think. Where could he be going overnight? His mother was too far away; he couldn't make a trip to see her in only two days. The only thing she could think of was that he was going away with *her.* And if he was, she might have driven him to it. She tried to shake that thought off. If he was seeing another woman, it wasn't because of her, a man couldn't be *driven* to another woman. Her head was aching and she felt absolutely miserable. She finally ate a little bit of her soup and then put the rest away. She couldn't face another silent encounter with Leo, so when he wasn't back at eight thirty, she went on up to bed.

Leo got up and left the house while GG was still in bed on Saturday morning. He got on the road as the sun was coming up, picking up a large coffee and a breakfast biscuit from a convenience store. He had spent some time on the phone at the office on Friday and made his plans for the weekend. He had several hours to drive and then he hoped to get some answers. He made good time and when he pulled into his destination, he had to grin at the massive motor home, with its awning strung with a string of colorful lights and the lawn chairs arranged around the firepit. He got out of his vehicle, stretching his stiff back as Margot and Don rushed out of the motor home to greet him. They both gave him heartfelt hugs and Don fished a couple of beers out of a cooler before they settled under the awning. Before long, Leo was telling them the whole story of the past few months for him and GG.

At first, Margot's eyes shone with tears as Leo described how grief-stricken GG had been over Bryce's unexpected death, but as his story went on, her expression began to change. When he got to the part, told carefully, of how she'd led him on and then rejected him, Margot actually shook her head in disapproval.

Leo said, "So I don't know what to think. I don't know if something's really wrong with her, or if I've screwed up by being so patient. I thought I was doing the right thing. She asked for time to heal and I thought it was only right to give it to her."

Margot said, "You were right at that time. And I think she did do some healing. What's going on now is entirely different."

Leo looked helplessly at her. "What could it be?"

Margot thought carefully about her words. "Leo, can you think of anything you've done or said that might lead GG to think that you're seeing another woman?"

He looked completely shocked, but Don didn't. "No! I would never do that!"

Margot held up a hand and said, "I'm not saying that you're doing it, I'm asking if there's something that could make her *think* that you could be. I don't think for a second that you would be unfaithful to GG, but it sure sounds to me like she thinks so. Think about it. The late nights working, Saturdays even, you said, right? Could she think that you haven't been working during all those times?"

Leo looked bewildered. "No, I *am* working. We've even talked on the phone a few times, my office phone, when I've worked late. She doesn't talk to me much about my time at work, she hasn't talked to me much for a long time. She's never even asked about the new engineer I've been training."

"That doesn't sound like GG," Don said.

"No, it isn't like GG. That's why I was so concerned about her, I wanted her to go have a physical and talk to Doc to see if maybe she was depressed, but she wouldn't have any of it."

"You're sure you can't think of anything? Someone new you've met, maybe?" Margot asked.

"No, only Connie, but GG's never even asked about her."

Margot pounced. "Who's Connie?"

"She's the new engineer."

Margot leaned forward and said, "The new engineer is a woman? Seriously?"

Recognition was slowly dawning on Leo's face. "Yes, and she's young and single."

"Oh, Leo, there's your answer."

"But GG doesn't know anything about her. Like I said, she doesn't talk to me about work anymore."

Don said, "Leo, believe me, she knows about her now. She found out somehow and it wasn't from you, which makes it even worse."

"Oh, shit," Leo said, gulping his beer. "Sorry, Margot. I never even thought about it."

"Because you never thought about your new engineer that way," Margot said. "But women can be really touchy about things like that, especially when they're in a vulnerable place like GG has been. And that surely explains the night before last."

"You're right. It was like she was getting revenge on me."

Don handed him another beer. "Well, one thing is good. It sounds like she has done some healing of her grief. Otherwise, this wouldn't be shaking her up the way it is."

Leo looked at both of them. "So what should I do now?"

Margot said, "It's time to put your foot down."

Leo was shocked once again. "What? Really?"

Margot nodded. "Yes, really. She's gone way too far with this. She could have just talked to you and neither of you would ever have gone through all this. It's time to put your foot down and put a stop to it."

Don nodded his agreement. "She's right. This is one of those times when you need to be firm with her."

Margot took her husband's hand. "It's time to get your wife back." She gave Don a little smile. "Now, Don, why don't you get the fire started and I'll go get the steaks seasoned?"

Leo enjoyed the rest of his evening with his in-laws and spent the night stretched out on the extra bed in the motor home. The next morning, Margot fixed bacon and eggs over the fire and they had a hearty breakfast before Leo started back to Boone.

Chapter 9

Leo had plenty of time to think things over on his drive back to Boone. In a way, he was relieved to think that mistaken jealousy was likely GG's biggest problem. It could have been something really desperately wrong with her and it wasn't. But the fact that after all their years together and everything they had been through together, she could really believe he was capable of being unfaithful to her hurt him very deeply. He knew one thing for certain; he was never going to let her get away with shutting down and refusing to talk to him again. It would *never* happen again. He had to accept a good bit of responsibility for letting her get away with that. Well, it was all going to be out in the open now and before the day was through, they were going to come to an understanding, whether GG liked it or not.

When he pulled into the garage, he sat there for a minute and took a few deep breaths. Then he got out of his vehicle and went into the house. It was quiet; no music or television was playing and he carried his bag upstairs and put his things away in his own bedroom where they belonged. There wouldn't be another night spent in the guest room. GG's car was in the garage, but he didn't find her in the house so he headed out to the back yard. Sure enough, she was out there weeding the flower bed. He stood there watching her until she looked up and saw him. The emotions that played over her face were fascinating. There was a blend of anger, then fear, following the little moment of happiness when she first saw him. She finally settled into an impassive expression spiced up by a little bit of defiance.

"You're back," she said, stating the obvious.

He walked over to her and held out his hand to help her up. "I'm back. And I'm ready to talk."

A flicker of dread crossed her face and then she said, "I'll go wash my hands. Would you like a beer?"

He gave her a brief nod. "That would be nice."

He followed her to the deck and she motioned to the chairs. "Have a seat, it's nice out. I'll be right back."

He raised an eyebrow as he watched her go in and then shrugged. If she wanted to have this conversation outside, it was okay by him. She might change her mind later, though. She was back in a few minutes with two beers and she settled into the chair beside him.

"I've had plenty of time to think things over and it's time for you to do some explaining," Leo said after he had his first sip of beer.

"*I've* got explaining to do?" GG asked.

"Yes, ma'am, you sure do. A lot of explaining. For weeks now, you've been on an emotional roller coaster. I don't know if you're going to cry or scream at me, from one minute to the next. And the stunt you pulled a couple of nights ago... that needs a lot of explaining. I might as well tell you, that night was the angriest I've ever been with you."

GG's stomach was rolling with dread. It had obviously

been the angriest she'd ever seen him and she'd provoked him on purpose. She tried to find a way to deflect what he'd said. "I think *you've* got some explaining to do. All these late nights at the office, for weeks and weeks now, and Saturdays too. What's really been going on?"

"Spell it out, GG. What do you think has been going on?"

She was silent for a moment as her cheeks turned pink. Then she burst out, "I don't *know!* But I do know that you haven't been spending all that time training a new engineer! Not an engineer like all the others. She's a *woman!* And you've spent all this time with her without ever seeing fit to mention that fact. And she's a young, single woman too! Now, why don't *you* do some explaining?"

His temper stirred, despite his efforts to clamp it down. "There's nothing to explain. She's the new junior engineer, she has a lot to learn, and I've been training her. You've gone weeks without wanting to have a bit of conversation about my job or anything else about me. You told me you needed time, you needed me to leave you alone so you could heal. I gave you what you wanted. Clearly, that was a mistake and it's one that I won't ever make again."

Outraged, she shouted, "My brother *died!* I did need time to heal!"

Grimly, Leo said, "It's long past time for you to stop using Bryce's death as an excuse."

GG gasped and jumped to her feet. "That's a horrible thing to say, Leo Beauchamp!"

"It's a horrible thing to do. And we're going back to the subject at hand. That subject is your behavior. First of all, just when and how did you find out that Connie is our new engineer?"

"I don't have to tell you anything!"

Now Leo was on his feet. He took her by the arms and held her firmly. "Oh, yes, you do. You're going to tell me everything and we're going to talk about it until it's all resolved, once and for all. And I am never going to let you shut me out again. Now, when and how did you find out?"

Bitterly, she said, "It was when I came back from my trip to meet with my new artists. I overheard it from two women in the grocery store."

Leo stood there, thinking it over. It made sense; that was the night she'd gotten hysterical when they were about to make love. And he'd blamed himself, thinking that he was rushing her. "GG, why didn't you just *ask* me about it? I'd have been glad to tell you all about Connie. I've never once had a thought about her that way and I can't believe that you would think I had."

She wasn't ready to see the hurt she had caused him. "How could I ask you if you were cheating on me with a younger, single woman? One who is pretty? If you were, you'd never have told me the truth, would you? That's not how it works."

"How do you know what she looks like?"

Self-consciously, she looked down before she blurted out, "Because I went to see. I saw the two of you sitting in a restaurant together. I watched you together."

"Oh, my God." Leo ran his hand through his hair in shocked frustration. "And what were we doing?"

GG was stubbornly silent.

"What were we doing, GG? While you sat in the restaurant watching us, what were we doing?"

She couldn't meet his eyes. "Eating lunch. There! Is that what you wanted me to say? But that wasn't the point. You never told me about her. You were spending time with this woman and you never once mentioned her to me. And you were so comfortable with her, it was like you were good friends or something."

"So you concluded that I was cheating on you with a

younger woman. Just like that, after the years we've spent together, you could actually *believe* that?" Leo was grim.

"I didn't... I didn't want to, but—"

"But what? But it was easier than just talking to me? I *love* you, GG. I was worried half to death about you. I've loved you for all these years and you believed this? And then, your plan to get back at me, that was what it was, wasn't it? You wanted to hurt me back."

GG was miserable, but she raised her chin defiantly. "Well, what would you do if it was me in your place?"

Leo said grimly, "I would have talked to you."

"So where did you go this weekend?" The suspicion was still in her eyes.

"I went to talk to your parents. I had to get some advice about what could be wrong and what I should do. They were the ones who told me that this was in your head."

GG's mouth dropped open in shock. "You went to see my *parents?*"

"Yeah, and you thought I was off spending the weekend with the other woman, didn't you?"

GG's face turned bright red and he knew he was right. "So now I'm going to take their advice."

His wife was suddenly terrified. Would he actually leave her? "What advice?" she gulped out the question.

"To put my foot down and be firm with you. I suggest you get in the house."

"No! I don't believe they told you that!"

Leo shrugged. "Okay, we'll stay right here in the backyard."

Seconds later, GG was bent over the table, Leo holding her there firmly with one hand while he smacked her bottom with the other. She kicked and squirmed, to no avail, and his hand came down harder and harder, peppering her bottom with stinging smacks.

"Leo, stop! Stop! Please, that hurts!" She tried not to make too much noise begging him. She was being spanked in the back yard where any of the neighbors could look over and see.

"Good, it should hurt. That's what spankings are for."

Unbelievably, his hand came down harder and faster and then, with GG gasping out her protests, he pulled down her shorts and panties and began spanking her bare bottom. A dozen spanks later, GG had forgotten about being quiet. She was wailing at the burn he was igniting in her bare bottom. Each slap burned like fire and he spanked her mercilessly, turning her pretty little butt a deep, fiery red. He covered every inch of her bottom and then he moved his smacks down to the sensitive spot at the top of her thighs and GG begged for mercy. Leo wasn't feeling merciful, though, and he kept on spanking her tender sit spot and even the backs of her thighs until his hand was sore and tired. With the last brutally hard smacks he administered, she burst into tears and sobbed, her struggles ending as she cried her heart out. He finally stopped and stood there, his hand still pressed to the small of her back, breathing heavily.

As GG's tears fell, Leo gave a weary sigh and turned and walked into the house. GG fought to get control of herself and then she realized she was still bent over the table with her bare, red bottom on display for anyone who wanted to look. She snatched up her shorts and panties and fled into the house. Leo had gotten himself another beer and was standing at the kitchen sink with his back to her. She was suddenly overcome with the enormity of the mistake she'd made and she dropped her clothes and crept over to him.

She fought for words and finally said, "Leo, Leo, I'm so sorry. I should have known better than to think you could ever do that to me. Please, please say you can forgive me."

He tipped his head back and took a swig of his beer, and when he turned, she could see in his face how deeply she had hurt him. Finally, he said gruffly, "GG, I love you. I've loved you from the moment I met you. That means I'll always forgive you. Maybe I could have ended all this sooner, if I'd just spanked you the night you pulled that nasty little stunt, but I was too angry. I didn't dare do it then. I might have hurt you, and I could never live with that."

She stared at him, tears still trickling down her face and he opened his arms and took her into his warm, strong embrace, the one she'd always been able to count on, and she nestled against him. She'd never been so happy to feel his arms around her and when she lifted her head, he kissed her, gently at first, then deeper and deeper, plundering her mouth with his tongue. She gave a little gasp of pain when he lifted her into his arms and carried her up to their room. He sat her on the edge of the bed, eliciting another little gasp and she pulled her top off over her head and then unfastened her bra and tossed it across the room.

Leo unbuttoned his shirt and pulled it off while GG worked at the button of his jeans. In moments, he stood there naked, his desire for her obvious. He groaned when she wrapped her hand around his erection, his need for her almost painful. When she lowered her head and closed her mouth over him, his legs trembled. She swirled her tongue around him, her hands stroking the full length of him, and he felt the weeks of frustrated desire building inside him. She sucked him strongly and cupped his balls in her hand, kneading them while she stroked him with the other hand.

"God, GG, you have to stop, I can't hold back."

She gave a little smile and said, "No, I don't. I want to take all of you."

She sucked him while she swirled her tongue around him, and he felt his control shatter until she was drinking every drop of his salty emission. He let out a shout, overcome by the sensation. They collapsed onto the bed together, Leo panting and quivering with the climax she'd brought him to. Gradually, his breathing slowed and he kissed her and murmured his love for her. She cuddled close to him and he began to stroke her soft, silky skin, playing with his fingers around her breasts, lightly pinching the rosy tips and making her squirm as his hand moved down her belly. He slid a hand under her and she winced as he gently squeezed her buttock, feeling the heat of her scorched skin. He spread her legs and cupped her pubis in his hand and he felt the wet heat between her thighs as she made a little hum of need.

Leo lowered himself so he could swirl his tongue around her tender, swollen nipples, sucking, nipping them, kneading her breasts and worrying the sensitive peaks with his tongue and teeth. GG moaned, feeling the ripple of heat through her belly and lower, where she felt swollen and wet and needy. Leo's fingers drifted down to the vee between her thighs and he explored her slick folds, finding her hard little center with his thumb before he plunged two fingers deep into her tight, sweet depths.

"Oh, oh, oh!" GG cried out, writhing beneath him in mindless pleasure. "Please, Leo, don't make me wait. I need you in me!"

She was stroking him as she begged, his member stiff and ready for her again. Finally, he pulled his hand away and she let her legs fall apart as he lowered himself between them. He pressed that rigid shaft against her sweet, hot opening and thrust himself into her with one smooth, strong plunge. GG cried out as he filled her and began to move within her. She rose to meet his thrusts and all her pent-up frustrations were tossed away as they rocked together in a deep, savage rhythm. She saw stars swirling around her as their movements grew faster and more intense. The climax building in her was blinding in its power, pushing her higher than she'd ever dreamed she could go, and when she exploded over the top, she screamed out his name, quaking and shuddering with the strong contractions of her muscles, milking him to another powerful climax. Her muscles quivered as she felt him throb and pulse inside her and a long shudder went down her whole spine.

They were gasping with the aftermath of their lovemaking, hearts pounding with the exquisite release, made stronger by the storm they'd just been through. They slowly came down from the heights of their passion and felt their bond strengthen once again. They lay there, pressed together, unwilling to move away from each other for a long time.

When they finally stirred, GG said softly, "Oh, God, Leo, I love you so much. How could I have been so stupid?"

He kissed her forehead and said, "Shh. It's over now and we're never going to let it happen again. I'm to blame too. I should have known better than to let you pull away from me like that. I won't ever do it again."

And she knew that he meant it. She would never be allowed to push him away again and she was grateful to know it. They could have lost each other and that was the worst thing that could ever happen to them. She felt her bottom burn when she moved and thought it was a reminder that she welcomed. Not that she wanted him to do it again, but she wasn't sorry that he had. Then a thought occurred to her.

"Oh, Lord, I almost forgot! The neighbors... the neighbors could have seen." She was mortified at the idea.

She felt the rumble of Leo's chuckle. "Well, if they did, I guess they didn't call the police. They'd have showed up by now."

"Oh, my God, that's so embarrassing!"

"I guess you should have gone in the house when I gave you the opportunity." He was still chuckling.

"Believe me, that's never going to happen again, either. Next time, I'll definitely be in the house."

"Oh, there's going to be a next time, huh?"

"Not if I can help it and never for a reason like this again," GG said fervently.

Chapter 10

Leo and GG kept their promises to each other. They found their way back to the closeness they'd shared for most of their marriage and spent hours talking together about anything and everything. Their lives weren't extravagant or particularly exciting; they still lived a simple, small-town existence that proved to be perfect for them. Their house was often filled with family and friends and it was always full of love and laughter. Leo was happy with his job, and he introduced GG to Connie, the junior engineer, and it turned out that GG liked her. She was a nice young woman with a generous heart and it was easy for GG to see why Connie and Leo became friends and worked together easily. And it turned out that Connie also had a boyfriend she adored and planned to marry someday. GG still loved running her shop. There was always new art to be discovered and new avenues to pursue.

GG and Leo also kept their promise to take a vacation every year, just the two of them. They chose a different place each year and always came back home renewed and relaxed. All in all, life was rich and rewarding and their bond constantly grew stronger and closer. They spent as much time with their grandchildren as they could, sometimes taking them camping, but most times the kids just wanted to spend time at their grandparents' house. They had busy lives with school and friends in the city and when they came to Boone, they were carefree and relaxed. Leo and GG talked a lot about how fast they were growing up. Shelby was still kindhearted and gentle and Savannah was still headstrong and impetuous. Carter was easygoing and funny and always had lots of friends wherever he went.

The girls were going to turn ten in a few weeks and Leo had been spending a lot of time thinking about the perfect birthday presents for them. One Saturday, after he finished mowing the grass, he sat down with GG to discuss it. They were sitting in the kitchen with cold glasses of GG's fresh lemonade and her homemade chicken salad sandwiches.

"We need to discuss what to get the girls for their birthdays," Leo said seriously.

"You've been talking about this for weeks," said GG. "What's so different this year? I usually pick out presents for the girls and you usually take care of Carter's."

"Ten is a very important birthday," Leo pointed out. "It's double digits!"

GG laughed. "That's true and it's really hard to believe they're almost ten already."

"I think I know the perfect gift for Savannah. It could be for both of them, but I think they should each have their own present and, besides, I don't think it's as perfect for Shelby as it is for Savannah."

GG looked at him curiously. "What is this gift you have in mind?"

He leaned forward and said, "A pony."

GG's mouth fell open in surprise. "A pony? How would we do that? We live in town."

"I've got everything all figured out," Leo said. "I talked to Mamie Harper and she said she'd be happy to have us board in their barn. They've got several empty stalls and she loves it when the kids are over there to see the horses. And she gave me some names of people who might have ponies for sale. One of them is perfect. He's a brown and white paint gelding, definitely smaller than a full-sized horse, but not a little tiny thing. He's had kids handling him all his life and he's well trained and gentle."

GG blinked at him. "I don't know what to say. You look awfully excited about this."

"You've seen Savannah's face when she's around the horses. It would be her dream come true. But it's not as perfect for Shelby. She likes the horses, but she's not crazy about them like Savannah is."

GG laughed. "It sounds like you've made up your mind about this."

"Well, no, I can't decide this unless you're okay with it."

"It sounds expensive."

"Look, I've listed every possible expense. I agree, it's kind of expensive, but that's the kind of thing we've worked for, isn't it? And look at this, it's a picture of the pony."

GG's heart melted as she watched her husband's obvious excitement. "What's his name?"

Leo knew he had her. "His name is Corky."

"Corky." She tried it out, imagining Savannah calling him. "That's a good name."

"But what about Shelby?"

GG said thoughtfully, "You're right, she likes the horses, but she's not like Savannah is. You know Shelby, she loves everything and she would never complain, but she should have her own birthday present."

Leo nodded. "That's exactly what I thought."

GG thought a little bit. "There's something I've been

thinking about lately. Rowdy is getting up in years. I hate thinking about it, but he won't live forever. He's still young enough to get along with other animals and I think it would be a good idea to get a second dog before Rowdy really starts to decline. I think it would be good for Rowdy and good for the girls. And Shelby would love that."

Leo gave her a loud, smacking kiss. "That's perfect! I knew you'd come up with the right thing."

"We'll have to talk to James and Allison about the pony and see if we can get the whole family here to celebrate the birthdays."

"We can do that tomorrow after church."

"I need to get ahold of the people we got Rowdy from and see what the status is on puppies. Oh, it'll be fun to have a puppy again!" GG loved puppies.

"It will," Leo agreed.

"And as soon as you get the okay from James and Allison, you can get the pony. If this is the pony you want. Did you want to shop around some more?"

"No, I looked at two others before this one and he's definitely the best of them. He's really gentle and I watched an eight-year-old girl ride him. He's the one I want for her."

GG grinned. "I think you're going to be as excited about it as she will. I just hope we can get a puppy in the right time frame. I really wouldn't want to get one from anyone but the Lawrences."

"No, I wouldn't either. If we have to wait, we have to wait. We can show Shelby what she'll be getting." Leo knew the dog would be staying with them as there was no chance of a Golden Retriever living in the high-rise apartment where James and Allison lived with their family.

GG laughed. "And Shelby's actually patient enough to understand if she has to wait. Savannah would be a whole different story."

"You've got that right! And Shelby will be excited for Savannah too, so it'll all work out."

"Savannah will let Shelby share her pony, as long as she knows that he's really hers." Savannah was impetuous and headstrong, but she had a generous heart too, especially for her identical twin.

James and Allison gave the okay for the pony after they had talked through Allison's reservations. She had always led a big city life and personally, she was scared to death at the idea of getting on a horse. But she knew her little daughter was becoming horse crazy and she also knew that Leo and GG would teach her to be safe. And one of James and her birthday gifts to their daughter would be a top-of-the-line riding helmet and boots. So they planned to have a birthday celebration at Leo and GG's house and GG got to work on the planning, conferring with Allison each step of the way.

They were in luck too. GG called Kate Lawrence, who raised Golden Retrievers, and who they'd gotten Rowdy from, and Rebel before him. They had a litter that had been born two weeks before and would be ready for their new homes right at the time they were planning the girls' birthday party. So far, only three of the seven pups were spoken for and since GG was a well-known customer to them, Kate promised GG could have the first pick. She would make her choice as soon as the puppies were developed enough to be active and playing with each other. After she'd chosen the active, outgoing pup, GG stopped by often enough to have lots of pictures of his development before Shelby was going to meet him. She would put them in an album for Shelby, the puppy's baby book, and she had no doubt that Shelby would add pictures to it over the years.

GG went with Leo two weeks before the birthday party to haul the pony over to the Harpers' and get him settled in. She could see instantly why Leo had been so sure that this was the pony he wanted for Savannah. The little girl who was giving him up cried when he left, but she had moved on to a horse and they weren't able to keep both of them. GG and Leo promised that they would take good care of him and the little girl waved until they were out of sight. Mamie Harper had given her approval before Leo had bought the pony and she was waiting at the barn to greet them and settle him into his new home.

On their way home a good hour and a half later, GG looked at Leo and laughed. "I think we're having just as much fun with this as the girls are going to have."

He grinned at her. "It *is* fun, isn't it? This is going to be the thrill of Savannah's life. I can't wait to see her face."

"And Shelby! She loves baby animals of all kinds, but a puppy is going to make her so happy."

"I just see one problem here," Leo said.

GG looked concerned. "What?"

"We're never going to be able to top this birthday for them. It's all downhill from here."

GG laughed and said, "You're probably right about that."

"You got plenty of pictures of Corky arriving at his new home, right?"

"I sure did. Savannah will have a baby book for him too. Even though he isn't exactly a baby, he's starting a new life with her."

When they pulled into the garage, Leo turned to GG with a serious look. "Do you think it's too much? The pony and the puppy?"

GG thought it over. "Maybe. But who cares? We're the grandparents, we're supposed to spoil them."

"So we're just carrying out our responsibilities."

GG grinned. "Right."

They went inside, laughing and talking over the plans for

the birthday party. A thought occurred to GG. "Do you think Carter will feel left out?"

Leo snorted. "Carter? He's the most well-adjusted, unselfish kid I've ever met. Not a chance."

GG smiled, her pride in her first grandchild showing. "He is, isn't he? He's just like his dad was."

"Except he's a little more ornery than James was. It's that quick sense of humor he's got."

"You're right. He thinks of things that never would have occurred to James. Do you think he's going to be a difficult teenager?"

Leo shook his head. "No, I really don't. I think he has too much fun without any interest in the kinds of things that would get him into trouble. He's a good kid and I think he's always going to be that way. He'll try out the usual things, but I don't think he'll get into any real trouble."

"I hope you're right. Things are so different for kids now than when James was young."

Leo laughed. "Yeah, but look how it was when you were a teenager. You tried your best to get into trouble."

"I did not!" GG did her best to look offended.

Leo nuzzled her neck and said, "Luckily for you, I was there to look out for you. There was a stretch of time when it took a lot of energy to keep you out of trouble."

"I was just curious. I wanted to know all about the world."

"Mm hm. Let me ask you, if one of the girls sneaked off and went to a music festival for the weekend in the age of free love and drugs, how would you feel?"

"They wouldn't do that. And they don't have those things anymore. And... but we went and we didn't get into any trouble, did we?"

"Nope, you didn't. It still amazes me to this day."

GG looked pensive. "I guess we were kind of lucky."

"Kind of! You were the luckiest two girls alive that weekend!"

She had to laugh at the look on his face. "Okay, I have to admit you're kind of right about that. I guess it was a good thing I had you watching out for me. But I had Bryce and Carl too. I was lucky I could even breathe with the three of you looking out for me."

"Uh huh. You always came up with a way to do what you wanted, didn't you?"

"I got the husband I wanted, didn't I?" GG gave him a smug grin.

Leo swept her up into his arms and said, "That's because I swept you off your feet and made you fall madly in love with me."

She giggled breathlessly as he nibbled at her earlobe, his breath tickling her and sending a chill down her spine. He carried her up to their bedroom and stretched out on the bed with her, both of them kicking off their shoes. Leo wrapped his arms around her and she snuggled close as he took her mouth in a lingering, leisurely kiss, tasting her and exploring her sweet mouth with his questing tongue. The kiss was passionate and playful as their tongues darted together, swirling around each other, then parting to taste each other's lips, then darting together to spar again. It went on until GG was whimpering softly, her body loose and hot, her arousal climbing.

They laughed and played as they gradually undressed each other, kissing each new area of exposed skin, stroking with their fingertips and teasing with their tongues. When they were finally nude in each other's arms, Leo stroked her throat, brushing his fingers down and over the swell of her breast.

"You're so beautiful," he murmured.

GG said lightly, "You must have your eyes closed."

Her husband growled his displeasure. "Are you asking for a spanking? I told you never to talk about yourself that way."

She snuggled closer and said, "You did. I'm sorry, sometimes I just can't believe that you still see me that way."

Leo said simply, "I see you that way because you are that way. Every line, every stretch mark or not-so-firm muscle is a thing of beauty to me. Each one stands for something you've lived through with me, an expression of our love together."

He stroked her breast with one finger, circling the hardened tip and pinching it gently. "This is where you nursed our son as a tiny baby. How could it ever be anything but beautiful?"

His words meant everything to her and she sighed in perfect contentment. "Oh, Leo, you are the perfect partner for me. I feel like we complete each other. How were we ever lucky enough to find each other?"

He looked into her eyes and said, "It was our destiny. We couldn't have stopped it if we'd tried. Fortunately, we weren't foolish enough to try." He lowered his head to her breast and closed his mouth over one swollen, aching peak to worry it with his tongue and suckle there until she was squirming beneath him. He took her hand and turned it palm up so he could kiss the inside of her wrist, his lips lingering against the pulse he could feel beating there. He nibbled his way up the inside of her arm until he reached her shoulder, kissing it and then moving to the hollow of her throat. Her skin was still as soft as it had been the day he'd married her and he stroked her belly, the muscles a little less tight than when she'd been a girl, and when his fingers brushed her there, he could see her in his mind, heavy with the child they'd created together. He moved down to kiss those precious muscles and GG gave a little, wordless moan of sheer pleasure.

She twined her fingers in his hair and gave herself over to the sensations he was kindling, little waves of arousal shivering through her body. He kissed the sensitive spot at the top of her thigh and sent chills skittering down her spine. She was ready for him, so ready, but neither of them was in a hurry, content to enjoy the pleasure that was heating their blood. When he pushed her legs apart and kissed the inside of her thigh, GG whimpered at the heat that swept over her and lifted her hips as he kept kissing her thigh, teasing her relentlessly. Finally, he lowered his head and she felt his hot breath on her before he lapped at her swollen, sweet center and she cried out at the intensity of the feel of his tongue in her most intimate places, circling the tender little bud and sucking gently until she arched her back and cried out again.

Leo licked and tasted her, loving the hot sweetness he found there and opening her to his fingers and mouth, driving her higher and higher on the waves of sensation that were sweeping over her. She was lost, her vision graying until it seemed there were stars bursting all around her and nothing existed for her but pleasure, building ever higher until suddenly Leo's hands and mouth were gone and she felt empty, just for a second. Then she felt the familiar weight of her husband as he lowered himself between her thighs and drove into her, making her arch against him, lifting her hips to meet his thrusts and groaning with the intense satisfaction of having him in her. They rocked together, climbing the peaks of their passion until they reached the top, teetering there until, with one more deep thrust, Leo pushed them both over and they tumbled through the intense spasms of their climax, shuddering and throbbing together.

The two of them held each other as their breathing gradually slowed and their hearts returned to their regular rhythm, as close as two people could be and glowing with the warmth of their love. GG wondered sometimes how it could still be so good after all these years, and Leo locked the memory away in his heart like he always did. They were complete, nearly one person, and they felt the rightness of their union once again, something they had always held precious. They drifted lazily on the warmth of their lovemaking until Leo's stomach growled and GG burst into giggles at him.

"Did you work up an appetite?" she asked teasingly, moving in his arms where they were still joined together.

"Mm, an appetite for you if you keep that up."

His stomach growled again and she said, "I think I'd better feed you or you won't have the strength for that again."

He kissed her and then let her go, chuckling at her as she wiggled her hips at him.

Chapter 11

Shelby's eyes were shining as she grinned at her grandmother. "I remember that birthday! Savannah does too, it was the best birthday we ever had. She loved that pony so much. He was the most important thing in her life."

GG snorted. "Right up until the time she discovered boys."

Shelby laughed. "Yes, you're right. She definitely did become boy crazy. And Rookie, he was the sweetest puppy and I loved him. He was my best friend for years. What a good dog!"

GG smiled. "He was a good dog and you took good care of him. He lived to be fifteen. I lost him right before you came back to Boone to live."

Shelby was smiling at the memories, shifting in her seat and reaching to rub at her back. "Have you ever thought about getting another one?"

"I think about it now and then. I just don't know if I'm up to raising another puppy."

Shelby nodded, still rubbing absently at her back. "I can understand that. A puppy is a lot of work."

GG gave her granddaughter an appraising look and commented, "I think maybe you've had enough for today. I can tell you're stiff and uncomfortable; you've been sitting there taking notes for long enough, and you're starting to look tired. Let's call it a day, and if you feel good tomorrow, you can come back for another session. If not, take a few days off. This story's not going anywhere."

Shelby's instinct was to argue, simply because she was so fascinated by her grandparents' story, but as her baby made his presence known again, she had to agree. "I hate to stop, but you're right, Gran. I'm ready to stretch out and get comfortable if this little one will let me."

Shelby started to put the notebooks and other things in order, but GG stopped her. "Just leave it, sweetie, it'll be there when we need it. You go home and get some rest. Would you like anything before you go? A snack? Water? Juice?"

Shelby laughed. "No, I'll just take a bottle of water with me and I'll plan on seeing you tomorrow."

GG insisted, "You call me tomorrow after you know how you're feeling. Then we'll decide."

"All right, Gran," Shelby said as she gave her grandmother a hug.

GG watched her leave and then closed the door with a sigh. Shelby wasn't the only one who was tired. And it wasn't just that; she had been sharing memories that had been precious to her for years. She wanted some time alone with her thoughts to take her time and relive some of those happy times she'd had with the love of her life. She felt surrounded by the warmth of the love they'd shared whenever she thought about him. He had always made her feel loved, safe, cherished. It had been a truly special love story and even though Leo wasn't physically with her anymore, she had never lost that feeling. She held it close to her heart always, and it kept him close to her.

When she and Shelby went on with the story, she was going to have to tell Shelby all about the adventure she and Leo had decided to go on when the twins were eleven. She settled down with a cup of tea and spent a long time thinking about it, reliving the crazy time. She actually laughed out loud a couple of times at the vivid memories and she couldn't wait to see her granddaughter's face when she shared it with her. Leo had truly given her a taste of the world when he'd planned that vacation! She was still smiling when she went into the kitchen to warm up some soup for her dinner. Carter's wife, Maggie, had brought it over the day before on her way home from the bakery she owned. She'd thought Maggie had looked a little bit excited about something; she'd have to quiz her about it when she saw her the next morning at the shop.

GG had finally slowed down her work at GG's Gems and considered herself to be semi-retired. Savannah was the perfect person to take over the management of the shop and she was doing an excellent job of it. They had part time help when they needed it and GG had discovered that she enjoyed having more leisure time. It meant that when the great-grandchildren began arriving, she'd have more time to spend with them. She had time to have lunch or dinner with her longtime friends, Sharon and Katie, and she found herself enjoying living at a bit slower pace. She finally had time to read the good books she'd never been able to get to and she had time to go through the boxes of cards, letters, and pictures she'd saved through the years. She was beginning to organize them in a series of albums and she knew that one day Shelby would take good care of them and pass the family history down to its younger members.

The next day Shelby called her, sounding energized and refreshed, and in the early afternoon, she arrived to continue with the story she was documenting. GG and Shelby made themselves comfortable and GG's tale began again.

Leo and GG's lives went on, busy, full, and happy, with work, family, and friends at the center of their world. And one day, Leo found a little kernel of an idea beginning to form in his brain. He pushed it aside at first, thinking that it was too exotic to really be practical or possible. But the thought refused to go away and he began to collect information and talk to people. As the days went on, he began to get excited about it and he finally became determined to make it happen. He examined and planned every angle until he had a real plan. All he needed was GG's okay.

One warm spring day, Leo bought a couple of really fine steaks and picked up a salad from a deli near his firm, along with a loaf of fresh bread, and got home from work early to make dinner for his wife. He put candles on the table with the fresh flowers he'd picked up. He turned on some of their favorite music and set the table. The steaks were seasoned and the grill was ready to be lit when GG walked in the door. Her mouth dropped open as she looked around at the scene Leo had set. He walked over and gave her a warm, probing kiss that took her breath away.

"What's the occasion?" GG asked, mystified.

Leo kissed her again and said, "That's a surprise. Why don't you go get comfortable and I'll pour the wine?"

She wanted to ask more questions, but she knew he wouldn't answer them until he was ready, so she went to change out of her work clothes and freshened up a little while she was at it. She was intrigued and couldn't even begin to imagine what kind of surprise her husband had in mind. When she returned, the candles were lit and the grill was heating up. Leo handed her a glass of wine and she took a sip.

"You're not going to give me a hint?" she asked.

"Nope, you'll just have to be patient," Leo said, taking a sip of his own glass of wine.

GG pouted. "You know I'm not very good at that."

Leo chuckled. "I know. That makes it more fun."

They enjoyed the delicious dinner on the back deck, which they had gotten screened in the year before. It was a lovely night, the food was excellent, as was the wine, and GG's curiosity was burning by the time they finished eating.

"Leo, you have got to tell me what's going on," GG finally exclaimed. "It's driving me crazy."

"All right, come with me." He blew out the candles and took her hand. "Bring your wine."

She followed him into the house and to the library, where there was a bag lying on the coffee table. "You know how we promised each other that we'd take a real vacation every year?"

GG nodded. "Of course. We've had some wonderful ones."

Leo said, "Well, I've decided that it's time we had a really special one. One that keeps a promise I made to you a long, long time ago."

GG was mystified. "What promise was that?"

"The promise to show you the world. I can't show you the whole world, but I can show you a part of it that we've never expected to see."

His excitement was obvious and GG didn't know whether to be excited or anxious. "What are you getting at, Leo?"

"I'm going to take you on a really special vacation; one that's exotic and unusual, one we've never thought of before."

"Where? Where are we going?"

He took the bag and pulled out a stack of glossy brochures. "We're going to Morocco."

GG lost her breath, her shock was so great. "Morocco? Really? Morocco?"

"Yes, look at these. We just have to plan the details of what we're going to do there; we've got to plan those together so we don't miss anything you'd like to do."

GG began to look at the exotic, beautiful photos and she caught his excitement quickly. "Leo, are you really serious? Can we afford this? How long are you talking about? Oh, my God, it's so gorgeous."

"Yes, I'm serious and, yes, we can afford it, and we'll be gone for twenty-two days." He grabbed her face in both hands and kissed her, hard. "GG, I've looked at every possible angle and planned for every possible problem. We've got to do it. We've got to do it now, while we're still young enough to really enjoy it."

"You're right about one thing. I never imagined that *this* was your surprise!"

They bent their heads over the stacks of paperwork and talked for hours, and by the time they went to bed, they knew they were going to Morocco. GG lay snuggled against Leo's shoulder and he said dreamily, "Just think, we could be lying under the stars in the Sahara desert."

"Oh, my God, I can't even imagine it. It makes me think of such exotic things. How did you ever think of it?"

"I'm not really sure. I just knew I needed to take you someplace really unusual and special and somehow Morocco popped into my head."

"I love it. I love you so much."

She felt his chest rumble with a chuckle. "I'll bet you say that to all the guys who offer to take you to Morocco."

GG laughed. "You got me. I do, I have to confess."

He hugged her tight and they drifted off to sleep spiced with exotic, desert dreams. GG woke early in the morning and stretched lazily, then snuggled deeper into the warmth of the bed until the memory of the night before struck her and her eyes popped open wide. Leo had already gotten out of bed and she sat up and called out his name. He opened the bathroom door, where he was getting ready for work and grinned at her.

"Good morning."

"Leo, it wasn't a dream, was it? Is it real?"

"You mean our little vacation we're planning? Yes, darlin', it's real." He laughed at the rapturous expression on her face.

GG flopped back down on her back and murmured, "We're really going to Morocco. I just can't believe it."

Leo laughed at her and said, "I'll call the agent today and get our dates set and a list of what we need to do. Tonight, we'll put it all on the calendar."

"Passports! We have to take care of our passports first." She sat up abruptly as she thought of the passports.

"I know, we need to renew them. Don't worry, we have plenty of time. And we'll put everything in the order that it needs to be done."

"Oh, Leo, I'm so excited!"

She looked so cute sitting there in bed, her face shining with excitement, that he had to go over to kiss her good morning. He lingered over the kiss until she whimpered and he gave a little growl.

"Maybe I should take a sick day and stay home with you," Leo said huskily.

"Mm, but I have to go to work, I have a couple of deliveries coming today. And, besides, you've never taken a sick day in your life."

"I could always start," he said hopefully.

GG laughed and said, "I think you'd better hold that thought until after work."

Leo sighed and kissed her once more. "I guess you're right."

The days flew by, busy with preparations for the trip, and GG's excitement continued to grow. They had decided that she would close her shop for a month and reopen it with a little celebration after they got back. She intended to try to ship some exotic things from Morocco back home to place in the shop and knew her customers would be fascinated by them. She read everything she could find about traveling to Morocco, what to expect, how to dress, what to see while they were there. It was going to be a dream vacation and she couldn't wait. At times, it felt like their departure day would never arrive, but it was finally very close.

Sharon and Jack, along with Katie and Tommy, came to have dinner with them a few nights before they left. They decided to go to the Burger Barn in a tribute to old times and they sat there late into the night, talking and laughing over their burgers and fries.

"I can't wait to hear the stories and see the pictures after you get back," said Katie. "What a wonderful trip!"

"Same here," said Sharon. "I think it's time for Jack and me to have a dream vacation. You two are inspiring us."

GG laughed and asked, "Where would you like to go for your dream vacation?"

Sharon said, "I think I'd like to go to Switzerland."

Leo said, "You two love skiing, don't you?"

Jack nodded and said, "We do. A winter vacation would suit us just fine."

"What about you, Katie?"

Katie's eyes were dreamy. "I've always wanted to go to Scotland. I've read about it for years and I'd just love to see it in person."

Tommy squeezed her hand. "But that's not the only place we'd like to go."

Katie smiled at him. "No, it's not. But that would be kind of a family vacation if we could swing it."

GG's curiosity was up. "Where are you talking about?"

"Vietnam," Katie said. "Danny has been talking about it more and more, and we've always wanted to see the country of his birth mother. It's a real dream of his and we'd love to go together."

GG was touched. "That's a lovely idea. Do you think you'll do it?"

Tommy said, "Yeah, I really do. We've been starting to plan it and save for it. Now, Scotland, I don't know if we'll be able to pull that one off."

Katie smiled quietly. "That's all right. I can keep dreaming about it, but it's much more important to go to the country that Danny came from."

Leo said, "Then you should go."

Sharon said, "Y'all are making me feel shallow. You're going to go see such exotic places and we just want to go skiing and drink hot toddies in front of a roaring fire."

They all laughed and Jack winked at her. "Hey, to each his own."

Leo grinned. "That's right. You do what makes you happy."

They laughed and teased each other late into the evening, and when they went their separate ways, they shared hugs all around and promised to get together again when Leo and GG got back. Even after all the years that had passed, they all remained close and enjoyed each other's company just as they'd done when they were young. GG smiled and rested her head on Leo's shoulder on the drive home.

"They're really special friends."

Leo kissed the top of her head and said, "The best. And they've always been the best, even with all the other friends we've made over the years, they've always been there, always the best."

"We're really lucky, aren't we?"

Leo said huskily, "The luckiest people in the world. And you're about to be even luckier because I'm going to take you to bed."

She laughed and turned up her face for his kiss.

Chapter 12

GG gripped Leo's hand tightly. They were only a few minutes from landing at the Casablanca Mohammed V International Airport and her heart was pounding with excitement. Their travel so far had gone off without a hitch and she couldn't wait for her first sight of Casablanca. Her face was glued to the window as they descended to the airport runway and she wasn't disappointed. She tried not to be impatient as they waited to file off the plane and then stop for a quick bathroom break before they went to claim their luggage. They were met by a driver who held a sign with their name on it, and soon they were on their way to their first hotel. It was just as beautiful as the pictures had been and they settled into their room with a happy sigh. Leo swept his wife into his arms and kissed her.

"We're really here!" GG squeezed him and lifted her face for another kiss. "Oh my God, Leo, we're in Casablanca!"

"Are you tired? Do you want to rest for a while?"

"Are you kidding? I want to go for a walk. I want to see some of Casablanca."

Leo laughed at her. "Okay, let's do it."

They walked through the streets of the neighborhood around their hotel, which they had picked precisely so that they could walk and enjoy the sights. They would be spending two full days in Casablanca and they had booked three half-day tours so they could see as much as possible. They had planned carefully so that they could experience as much of the exotic country as they could while they were there. The streets were bustling with activity, and they bought fruit from a vendor and just drank in the atmosphere. The hotel had taken care of dinner reservations for them and their first day in Morocco was absolutely magical. By the time they returned to their hotel after dinner, the day had caught up with them and they slept dreamlessly until their alarm sounded early the next morning.

GG and Leo took turns snapping pictures, fascinated by the historical sites they visited, the architecture, the markets, the call to prayers. It was everything they had imagined and more. When they moved on by train, they were headed to Marrakesh and more wonderful sights. They saw mosques and synagogues, they visited museums and local art galleries, they spent hours in the fresh markets. They saw snake charmers, fortunetellers, poets, and storytellers in the historic square in Marrakesh. They visited the Jardin Majorelle, two and a half acres of exotic gardens, and the Berber Museum. They spent hours shopping in the souks of Marrakesh, the marketplace that sold literally everything. They spent the evening in the open-air square full of food stalls and entertainers. They sampled all the local food that they dared to try and then chose a roof top terrace to sit on and enjoy the sights.

After Marrakesh, Leo and GG traveled to the Sahara Desert, where they had reservations for a luxury camping experience. They learned to bake sand bread and rode camels. They took a 4x4 out across the desert and explored the dunes. They had delicious food for every meal and lay on blankets on the sand after night fell, gazing through the crystal-clear sky at the stars. It was truly magical and they loved every minute of their time in the desert.

After their stay in the desert, Leo and GG had opted for a different experience altogether and they traveled on to Fez, where they visited the city's ancient, walled medina. The maze of streets, alleys, tiny stalls, donkeys pulling carts, and hordes of people was an incredible experience. They visited the square dedicated to metalwork and went to see a holy Islamic shrine. They walked through the henna souk and GG had a tiny piece of henna artwork done on her cheek. They bought oranges and walnuts, along with a freshly baked baguette at the fresh produce stalls in another part of the medina and took them to the ParcBoujloud to sit and eat their makeshift picnic. They walked to the Merenid Tombs, where they watched the sun set over the medina, and then they walked back and found a restaurant at the gates of the medina for dinner. It was a full day and when they returned to their hotel room, they were so tired that they tumbled into bed as soon as they had showered, sleeping dreamlessly until the sun rose.

Their dream vacation was nearly over, and they spent their last day shopping for things to take back with them. GG had already shipped several boxes back to her shop and the two of them enjoyed one last genuine Moroccan dinner and then made slow, luxurious love in their room, with the warm breeze wafting over them and the sounds and scents of the city drifting up from the streets below. It had been a wonderful, magical time and they had taken hundreds of pictures and made memories they would never forget. When they drifted off to sleep, they dreamed of the star-studded desert sky and slept peacefully.

GG and Leo went back to Boone and life as usual, except that GG, especially, tended to zone out in a daydream, reliving the magic of their trip to another world. She had all their pictures developed and waited impatiently for her boxes to arrive from Morocco. They had James and Allison and the kids over to see the pictures and hear the stories and they gave them the souvenirs they'd brought back for them. Savannah, especially, was fascinated by the pictures of the exotic places. She couldn't get enough of them, and GG smiled, thinking of the book of professional photos of the country that she had put away for Savannah for Christmas. All three of the kids were beyond impressed at the photos of Leo and GG riding the camels.

Savannah declared, "Someday I'm going to go to Morocco and I'm going lots of other places too, all over the world."

GG thought back to when her greatest wish was to see the world and watched her granddaughter and thought that she just might do it. She could imagine Savannah becoming a world traveler without any stretch of the imagination at all. Shelby, on the other hand, was captivated by the pictures of the children, fascinated by the clothes they wore and the places they lived. Carter just thought it was the coolest adventure he'd ever heard of, especially sleeping in a tent in the desert. James and Allison had done their share of traveling, but Morocco was a place they'd never gone and they were beyond pleased that Leo and GG had gotten to experience it.

When GG's shipments arrived, she had more fun at work than she'd had in a long time, arranging and staging the exotic and unusual gifts, fabrics, and trinkets she'd sent back. It gave a decidedly international flair to the shop, and as the word got out, her regular customers had to come check it out. She sold out of nearly all her Moroccan items in little more than days and was grateful that she'd gotten some information on how to order more. She'd kept back a little something for Sharon and Katie and they went to dinner one Saturday and pelted GG with questions about the trip. She gave them their gifts and showed them her pictures and answered all their questions. And she was thrilled to hear that Katie and Tommy were proceeding with their plans to visit Vietnam.

They spent more than three hours at the restaurant and finally parted with hugs and promises to do it again soon. They left a very generous tip for their patient waitress, and GG walked into the house with a smile on her face. Leo grinned when he saw her.

"I don't have to ask if you had a good time," he said, "it's all over your face."

GG kissed him and sighed happily. "It's good to have such awesome friends."

Leo poured her a glass of wine and they sat down together. "Okay, tell me all about it."

They talked and laughed and drank a bottle of wine and stayed up much later than they usually managed, even on a Saturday night. And they slept in the next morning, skipping church for once and sharing a lazy day, just the two of them. GG made French toast and Leo fried the bacon and they ate on the back porch, knowing that the warm weather wouldn't be around for much longer. They read the Sunday paper and finished the pot of coffee, and GG had the thought that it was a perfect moment and she'd like to freeze it in her memory. She gave herself a mental shake, wondering at the bit of melancholy she felt. Then Leo leaned forward with a conspiratorial look on his face.

"If you could do it again, where would you want to go?" he asked.

GG was confused. "Do what again?"

"Go on a really special vacation. I think we should do it again next year."

"But this was a once in a lifetime trip. I don't expect to do it again."

Leo took her hand and said, "I watched you, I saw how much it meant to you to see a piece of the world like we did. It was amazing, and I remember how much you always wanted to see the world. And the thing is, I loved it too. It was one of the most special things we've ever done. Let's do it again."

The idea took her breath away. "But, Leo, it's so expensive. Could we really afford it?"

"I've been saving ever since the twins were born, for something special for here. I always thought it would be a pool. One of the best, in ground, with all the extras like a heater. But the kids have already started to go their own ways. They've got school and friends and social activities and they're going to spend less and less time here. Savannah is already starting to like boys better than her pony. And that's okay; it's normal. They have to grow up. But I don't think it's a really smart thing to do, putting all that money into a pool for them, knowing that they're not going to use it the way I visualized when I started saving for it. And I sure don't want to spend all my spare time keeping up a pool that isn't being used, not the way it should be. So, yes, let's spend that money on us. Let's do it, let's see more of the world."

His excitement was easy to see. "Oh, Leo…"

"You'd love it, wouldn't you? And before you ask, I'd love it too. I'd love nothing better. I had the best time and I really want to do it again. Come on, think about where you'd love to go."

"What about you? Isn't there someplace you've always wanted to go?" GG asked.

"You know where I've always wanted to be? With you. Wherever you are, that's where I want to be. You choose."

The swell of love in her heart would have brought her to her knees if she'd been standing. This man was her everything; she had never imagined back when she was eighteen years old and head over heels in love with him just how deep their love would grow. They were truly blessed. She took a deep breath and said, "There is a place I've always wanted to go. Ireland. The countryside, the history, the farms, the churches, the pubs, the music and the people. It's always sort of called to me. I would love to go there."

Leo's smile grew broader. "That's a place I'd love to see too. We're going to do it. We'll start planning it now." He popped up out of his chair and said, "Come on, lass, we're going to find a pot o' gold." He swept her up in his arms and carried her into the house and up to their bedroom.

GG giggled helplessly as he laid her on the bed and raised her top, peeking lasciviously underneath. "There's no pot o' gold there," she gasped, laughing.

"Ah, then, I'll keep looking. 'Tis here somewhere." He was undressing her as he spoke, his hands caressing and tickling and his lips soon following his hands.

GG sighed and thrilled to his familiar touch, the shudder that ran down her spine, the gooseflesh that rose on her skin. His touch set her on fire and she was suddenly beset by an urgency that made her pull off his clothes and lay her hands and mouth on his skin. They explored each other's bodies as if they were young again, touching, tasting, kissing and nipping. When they came together in the familiar dance of passion, there was just as much desire as when they were newlyweds. They climbed the heights of desire, their bodies thrilling as they drove toward fulfillment and then they cried out together as they burst over the top, shuddering and throbbing together as they reached the stars.

His heart pounding, Leo stroked her hair and murmured in her ear, "God, GG, it's still so good, every time. I love you more each and every day."

She snuggled even closer to him. "Leo, you are everything.

Everything I need, everything I want. I love you. I don't know how it can keep growing, but it does."

They lay there for a long time, talking and planning, laughing and imagining, until they heard the doorbell ring.

"Shh!" Leo whispered. "They'll go away in a minute."

GG was giggling and the doorbell rang again. While his wife giggled helplessly, Leo tiptoed over to the window and peeked out around the curtain. After watching for a minute, he came back to the bed.

"All clear. They're gone."

GG asked, "Who was it?"

"Just Pastor and his wife."

"Leo! We just ignored the pastor and hid here, naked, in bed?"

He said solemnly, "It was probably better than answering the door, considering. They must have missed us in church."

GG collapsed in uncontrollable laughter. "Maybe they'll pray for us."

"I hope if they do, they pray for food for us. I'm starving."

"Put some clothes on," GG instructed. "Then we can raid the refrigerator."

When they got downstairs after freshening up and dressing, GG went to the kitchen and Leo went to check out the front door. He joined her a minute later, carrying a covered dish and a note. She turned around and saw him and her mouth dropped open. Leo set the dish on the table and opened the note.

"Leo, what is that?"

He read quickly. "We're going to burn in Hell for sure. They were worried at church that we might be under the weather, so they brought us a casserole from the carry-in they had after the service."

"Oh, shit, I forgot this was the Sunday for that. I signed up for a salad."

Leo looked hopeful. "Well, did you make it? It'd go good with this casserole."

"Stop it," GG scolded, then burst into giggles again. "It's a good thing they didn't know why we were really skipping church."

Leo said, "Now, God created men and women to do exactly what we did together."

His wife fixed him with a stern look. "But not during church."

He walked over and nuzzled her neck. "We'll make it up to them at the next carry-in. I'll even help."

"You're so rotten." GG's breath quickened as he nibbled at her earlobe and she said weakly, "Well, I suppose that would work. What kind of casserole is that, anyway?"

Leo peeked under the cover and said, "I don't know; you know more about those things than I do."

GG stepped over and took the lid off the casserole. "Oh, that's Grace Vance's scalloped potatoes and ham. It's one of my favorites. And it's still warm. I'll toss a salad."

"That's my girl," her husband said with a grin as he gave her a little pinch on the backside.

The salad and casserole hit the spot just beautifully on that Sunday afternoon.

Chapter 13

Leo and GG's second dream vacation was much different than the first one, but it was just as magical. They spent a couple of nights in a bed and breakfast in a little village surrounded by miles of pasture and farmland, the rolling green pastures bordered by stone walls. They ate at the local pub and were welcomed in on Friday night when the pub was full of locals playing music, singing, and dancing. They explored historical old churches and hiked to rugged cliffs overlooking the waves that crashed against the rocky shore. They went to St. Patrick's Cathedral, visited ancient castles and museums, and immersed themselves in Ireland's history. It was like stepping into an older, simpler time and GG found it to be spellbinding and hauntingly beautiful. Again, she sent boxes back to the shop and carried home mementos to family and friends.

When they got back home to Boone, it took a few days to settle into reality again, just as it had after Morocco, but they were energized and refreshed once again. They had made precious memories, documented by lots of pictures, and had stories of people they had met and things they had seen that fascinated the grandkids especially. And shortly after they got back, Katie and Tommy set off on their trip to Vietnam with Danny and Li. When they got back, it was clear that the trip had been an amazing experience for them all. They had connected with the heritage that Danny had never gotten to know and seeing the place where his mother had been born and lived most of her life was a very special connection for him. And it was good for his wife too; her grandmother had been Vietnamese, although her grandfather was American. Li had always heard stories and seen pictures of her grandmother's homeland but it was all new to Danny.

As soon as they settled back in, Leo and GG began to plan their next trip. It had quickly become a tradition for them and the planning was half the fun. They talked and talked over where to go next. Leo was pushing for an African safari, while GG was fascinated by Australia and New Zealand. They sat in front of the fireplace with travel brochures strewn around them and Leo had to laugh at the exuberant expressions on GG's face as she talked about the trip she had in mind. He finally grabbed her and pulled her onto his lap.

"If you have your heart set on Australia and New Zealand, then that's what we'll do. We've got the rest of our lives to see Africa. Besides, we've been to Morocco, right?"

"Really? We can really go to New Zealand? It's so beautiful!" GG was beyond excited and she snaked her arms around him and lifted her face for a kiss.

And so they made plans for a New Zealand and Australia vacation. Going on their exotic vacations had added an extra bit of spice to their lives, and Leo was supremely pleased that he was able to give GG a taste of what he had promised her so many years before. In the fall, they celebrated their fortieth wedding anniversary with all their family and friends. They still had GG's parents and Leo's mother with them, and although Leo's mother wasn't well enough to join them, both his sisters did. GG's parents were looking for a place to settle; they'd had enough of living in the motorhome and found themselves going back over and over to South Carolina. Leo was planning to retire at sixty-five, so he had two more years of work to go and GG planned to find a manager for her shop and shift to semi-retirement.

The party went on late into the night and GG's parents finally went to their home on wheels for the night while Leo's sisters and their husbands spent the night in the girls' old rooms, which had been converted to guest rooms long before. James and Allison and the kids stayed too and when GG and Leo cuddled under the covers, he had to chuckle.

"This isn't the most romantic way to spend the night of your fortieth anniversary," he said softly.

"I think it's wonderful. We'll have all the privacy we want after this weekend is over, but it's so good to have everyone here."

He gave her a long, tender kiss and she melted against him, giving a little hum of pleasure when he kissed her eyelids and nuzzled her neck.

"Happy Anniversary, GG," he whispered.

"Happy Anniversary, Leo," GG answered, her eyes already growing heavy. It had been a long but wonderful day. And they fell asleep in each other's arms.

Shelby sighed, her eyes shining with the appreciation of her grandmother's story. "These are things that I can remember, Gran. The vacations, we were fascinated by the stories you told about them and we loved looking at the pictures. And I remember that party too."

GG smiled. "It was a good party. And Savannah had a

good time, it was like she forgot to be bored by the small-town festivities."

Shelby laughed. "Well, she had a new outfit to show off. And there was always a chance that there would be a new boy to focus on."

"She was boy crazy, wasn't she?"

"That's a fact. But one reason she was always okay with coming to Boone was those vacations. She absolutely loved the pictures and the stories. And she always swore that someday she'd go to all the places you went and more."

GG said, "Well, she kept that promise. Savannah has really seen the whole world."

"Yes, she has. But she still ended up back here like the rest of us."

"I never really thought it would happen. I always hoped it would, but it was a slim hope."

"Well, you did a good job of making it happen," Shelby said with a laugh.

"I did scheme a little. But if it hadn't been for Ben, I still don't think she would have stayed."

Shelby nodded. "They're so good together. Ben is the perfect husband for Savannah. They've been genuinely happy ever since he brought her back here from France."

GG's smile was peaceful. "Are you hungry?"

Shelby laughed. "I can honestly say I'm always hungry."

"Then let's take a break."

Leo and GG's forty-first anniversary was celebrated in Australia during another beautiful, magical vacation. They saw as much as they could manage in their three weeks' stay and quickly realized that there was enough in that part of the world to see that they could have spent twice as long there and still not seen it all. On the flight back home, they talked about all their vacations and the wondrous things they'd been lucky enough to see and experience. GG laid her head on Leo's shoulder and snuggled close as he kissed the top of her head.

"But with everything we've seen, home is still the best place," GG murmured with a happy sigh.

"It is. Because it's our home and we're there together. I have to confess, I'm ready to get back there," Leo said.

"I am too. I'm ready to see the family."

When the family all came for the post-vacation get together, it was better than ever. GG looked around at the noisy, happy group and realized that no exotic destination could ever top being right in their home, surrounded by their family and friends. They were truly blessed.

Leo and GG settled back into life as usual and spent a lot of time discussing, imagining, and planning what they would do after Leo retired. He was looking forward to having time to pursue a new hobby and GG suggested cooking lessons, which made him laugh and tell her that he was thinking more of something like woodworking.

"You do what makes you happy," GG said, laying her head on his shoulder where they sat one evening on the couch.

"Mm, I know exactly what that would be." He lifted her chin and kissed her lingeringly. "Let's go upstairs early." And the two of them locked the doors and climbed the stairs, stopping for kisses along the way.

It was a pleasant spring day, and Allison had brought Savannah to spend the weekend with her grandparents. She was going through a rebellious stage and had lost her privileges for the weekend, when she had hoped to be going to a party with older kids than her crowd. But she'd been found out and so, after some discussion, James brought her to Boone, where there was no way she could sneak out to the party. GG had invited her to go to the shop with her, but Savannah chose to sulk in her room instead.

"I'm sorry she's being unpleasant," GG told Leo as she was getting ready to leave.

Leo said cheerfully, "Don't be. It's a normal part of being a teenager. She'll get over it in time and if she stays up there pouting all day, it's probably not the last time it'll happen. You go on and don't worry about us. I could use a quiet day. I've got a little bit of a headache."

"Oh, no, are you feeling all right otherwise?" GG asked anxiously.

"Yes, I'm fine, it's just a little headache. I'll take an aspirin and read the sports section."

"Well, you call me if you start feeling worse."

He laughed at her. "Now, stop it and go on to the shop." He gave her another kiss for good measure and shooed her out the door.

Leo checked in on Savannah a little later, and since she still refused to come out, he went to the den with his newspaper and a woodworking magazine he had picked up. Several hours later, GG came into the house from the garage, humming in satisfaction at the day she'd had. The house was quiet and she chuckled to herself. Savannah was much too stubborn to give in when she was sulking, although if anyone had been able to coax her out of her mood, it would have been her grandpa. She put her bags down and went looking for Leo.

GG didn't see him the first time she went into the den. She had to go back again and walk around in front of the couch, and that was where she found him, on the floor in front of the couch. Her eyes widened and she rushed over to him, frantically calling his name and fumbling for a pulse or any sign of breathing. She breathlessly called 911 and started CPR, and a sharp, stabbing pain pierced her heart as she tried mindlessly to bring him back. When the paramedics arrived, they went through all the right moves, but she knew without a doubt that he'd been already gone when she got home. The commotion was finally enough to bring Savannah out of her room and she stood off to the side, her face frozen in horror.

The next few hours were the worst nightmare GG ever lived through. She was paralyzed with grief, unable to even cry. She came to herself long enough to take Savannah in her arms to comfort her, but there was no comfort to be had. In one afternoon, all their lives changed forever. Katie heard the call on the ambulance radio and she came as quickly as she could and she stayed with GG while they loaded Leo up and took him away. James and Allison were on their way and Katie made phone calls for GG, starting with Sharon, who was there within an hour. Don and Margot were booking a flight and would be there as soon as possible, and it wasn't until GG had to speak to Leo's sisters that she broke down. Sharon took the phone and talked to Ginny, who promised to take care of their mother, and GG wept, deep, wracking sobs on and on until she felt she would never produce another tear.

"Oh, Leo, how could this happen?" And fresh tears began to flow. Doc Harper prescribed a sedative for her and when she finally couldn't cry any longer, she fell into an exhausted sleep.

The days of the funeral were a blur of pain to GG and fresh pain stabbed her when she saw the sorrow of her son and his family, but she couldn't do anything for them. She went through all the right motions, but she was an empty shell of herself. The idea that Leo could be gone forever was incomprehensible to her. They were one together, they were going to grow old together, see their great-grandchildren, rock together on the front porch. This was just wrong and she couldn't believe it was real. She couldn't feel anything but pain and emptiness. Margot offered to stay on with her daughter, but GG refused.

"No, Mom, Dad needs you."

Margot looked desperately worried. "But, honey, I think maybe you need me more."

"No." GG gave her mother a weary look. "But there's something you can do for me. Be with Daddy, don't miss any more time with him. It's the most precious thing you can have, time with him. Please, go home and take care of each other."

She wouldn't hear of anything different, so finally her parents flew home. James and Allison and the kids had gone home a couple of days after the funeral. They had to get back to jobs and school and life. And finally, the big house was empty and GG looked around it with an exhausted sigh. It was as empty as her heart, the kind of aching, bone deep emptiness that she knew would never leave her. And that night she cried herself to sleep, holding Leo's ratty bathrobe that he refused to give up because he said it was so comfortable. She hugged it close to her chest and she could smell his familiar scent, and at some point the weariness overcame her and she slept.

Chapter 14

The days dragged by and GG's shop remained closed. She lost too much weight and she lost her joy for life, the joy that had always been such a part of her. She spent all of her time longing for her lost love and wishing hopelessly that none of it was true. One day Katie came to try to talk to her, but even though GG gave her the right answers, there was no spark in her eyes. She was lost without Leo. Katie and Sharon met for coffee and talked over their worry for their friend.

"I couldn't reach her," Katie said. "It's like only her physical self is there, her heart is gone."

"Did you try to talk to her about what Leo would want her to do?" Sharon asked.

"No, I just couldn't do it, not yet. The only thing I know she *does* feel is pain and I was just afraid I'd make it worse." Katie looked helpless.

"You think I should try?"

Katie gave a little shrug. "I don't see how it could hurt. It's not good now."

"And she doesn't have any plans for getting back to work?"

"No, she just said she's not ready yet."

"All right, I have to try. I'll give her a few days since you were just there, but somehow we've got to reach her. She's lost way too much weight and those dark circles under her eyes..."

Katie said, "I know. I'm really getting worried about her."

But before Sharon got the chance to go see GG, their family attorney called. "GG, I know you're going through the worst loss imaginable, but I have some paperwork I need to go over with you and have you sign, and I have something for you, too."

GG sighed. "Can't we put it off for a while?"

"No, I don't think that's a good idea. I know you and Leo left everything to each other, trusting each other to take care of your family, but there are a few loose ends to tie up. Can you come in on Friday?" He was gently insistent.

"I... yes, I guess so. What time?"

"I'm free at ten, will that work for you?"

GG sighed again. "I guess so. I'll see you then."

When she walked into the attorney's office, his secretary was shocked at GG's appearance. She hid it well, but GG was obviously suffering. It was only a minute before the attorney opened his door to usher her in. He offered her something to drink and poured her a glass of ice water from the pitcher sitting off to the side.

"You know that Leo made smart investments over the years. It was important to him to provide for his family and he did a good job of it."

GG smiled faintly. "He was always fiddling with the accounts, watching the stock market and switching stuff around."

"He did well. He took some long shots, but when they paid off, he always put the majority of the money into a safe, steady growth fund."

"I didn't know a lot about all that. I trusted Leo to take care of those things."

Glenn smiled at her. "Your trust was well founded. So, without Leo, I assume you don't want to mess with making risky investments?"

"No, I wouldn't know where to begin. Just put it where it's safe."

Glenn went through some of the stack of paperwork in front of him. "Then I'll need a few signatures. Eventually, when you reach the right age, you'll have to start drawing money out of the accounts. It's the law and it'll provide for you if you want to retire. You won't have to worry."

GG looked listless. "That's good, I suppose."

"It is good. Many times when a person is lost unexpectedly, everything is a mess. People always think they have plenty of time. I don't think Leo thought that way."

"What do you mean?"

Glenn said, "I had a conversation with Leo once when he told me that he never trusted that he would have as much time as he wanted with you. So he had to make the best of whatever he did have. He told me to treasure the time I have with my wife and I know that that's the way he lived, treasuring his time with you."

There was a sheen of tears in GG's eyes and she felt like she was struggling to breathe. "Oh, God, Glenn, I miss him so much."

"I know. What do you think Leo would say to you if he saw you right now?"

"He... I don't know."

Glenn leaned forward and asked gently, "Do you think it would make him unhappy to see you struggling this way? To see you not taking care of yourself?"

GG instantly knew exactly what Leo would have to say to

that. He'd probably be burning up her butt for her. But Leo was gone.

Glenn studied her face. He could practically read her thoughts. "Let's get these papers signed. Then there's one more thing to cover." He guided her through signing the stack of paperwork and then he set it aside. "We'll send you copies of all of this, and now I have one last thing." He opened his desk drawer and pulled out an envelope. "When you and Leo got ready to go to Morocco, he brought me this. He said that he couldn't shake the fact that accidents can happen and travel can be risky. So, if anything were to happen to him, he wanted me to give you this. You can open it at home, in privacy. It's personal, not a financial paper."

GG's hand trembled uncontrollably as she took it. "Oh, my God," she whispered.

Glenn patted her hand and said, "GG, go home and heal. Think about the memories you have, the closeness you shared. Do you believe that Leo is in a good place?"

She nodded violently. "Yes. He has to be."

"Then I believe that he's watching you and worrying about you. Take care of yourself and the family you have left and make Leo as proud as he's always been of you. Doesn't he deserve that?"

GG swiped away her tears and said, "I'll try. I will, but it just hurts *so much.* I just want him back so badly."

Glenn said gently, "I know you do, but that's the one thing you can't have. So make him proud, love your kids and grandkids for both of you. He needs you to do that for him."

When he stood and came around the desk to shake her hand, GG hesitated and then gave him a hard hug. She didn't know how to find the courage she was going to need, but she knew she had to. GG went home and laid the envelope on the table. She wanted to rip it open and devour every word, but she was scared to death to open it at the same time. She replayed every word Glenn had said to her in her mind. Had Leo had some kind of premonition that he wasn't going to live long? How could that be? He'd been in perfect health, there had been no indication that something was wrong with him. That was why it had been so shocking when he'd gone the way he did. Doc Harper had reassured her that he firmly believed Leo's death had been practically instantaneous. The shock of it made her think of her brother, Bryce, and the suddenness of his death. GG paced back and forth, her gaze returning again and again to the envelope. She picked it up several times and laid it back down again. Her head ached and she told herself that she couldn't read it until she got rid of the headache and was more focused. Then she told herself that she couldn't possibly wait to read it and still, she couldn't bring herself to open it.

She thought, *Leo had something to tell me. Important enough to write it down and have his lawyer hold it for him. I don't know how it could possibly make anything better now, or help me in any way, but it's something he felt was important to tell me. I have to read it, I have to give it a chance. He knew me better than anyone in the entire world ever did, even my own family. I have to read it.*

She pulled out a chair and sat down at the table, holding the envelope. The empty pit of her stomach was gnawing with the desolate pain of her loss and she held the envelope close to her face, hoping to catch his scent. It was silly, but she laid the envelope back down and hurried upstairs to get the bathrobe she'd been sleeping with every night. She held it close and breathed his strong, familiar scent as she walked back downstairs. She carried the envelope and the bathrobe into the library, where she curled up in the corner of the couch and turned on the lamp on the table beside her. She held the bathrobe on her lap and took a deep breath as she stared at the envelope. Finally, she used a letter opener to carefully slit it open. She pulled the folded sheets out and laid the envelope aside. GG carefully unfolded the letter and gazed through a sheen of tears at his familiar handwriting.

My GG,

If you're holding this now, then something has happened to me. Maybe it was unexpected or maybe I was a hundred years old. I kind of hope that's the case. The point is, I know I'm not with you anymore, not physically. And I'm sorry for that. I hoped you would go first so that you didn't have to bear the pain I know you're feeling now. I know it because I've imagined so many times what it would be like if I ever lost you.

Do you remember when we first met, at the Vietnam protest? I know you do because we've talked about it. I saved your butt that day and you were sassy enough to give me crap about how high handed I was with you and Sharon. At least Sharon thanked me for helping you two. Not you, though. It made me laugh later and you know what else it did? It meant I couldn't get you out of my mind. You were just a spoiled, impulsive kid but I couldn't forget you and I really wanted to see you again. It took a while, but it happened.

You should have seen your face when you saw me and realized who I was. But I guess it was meant to be from the beginning, wasn't it? We had our ups and downs but before long, I knew that I would never love another woman again even if you never gave me the time of day. You were my real, honest-to-God soulmate. Before you, I don't know if I believed that such a thing really existed.

The day we were married was the beginning of my real life. You were always the center of it. I loved everything about you, even at those times when you could make me mad. We went through our hard times, didn't we, really hard ones, but we managed to come through them together and each time we were stronger for it. One of my very best memories is what you looked like pregnant with James. You were the most beautiful creature I'd ever seen in my life.

And look how he grew up! He's a man to be proud of, he's a man who treasures his family. That's the most important thing he can be. And

Carter and the girls, who could have imagined how wonderful it would be to have grandchildren? They're the greatest blessing we could ever have been given.

It's become really important to me to go some of the places with you that you've always wanted to go. I know how much your dream meant to you, your dream of seeing the world. And the world is magnificent when I look at it through your eyes. I'm so glad we're able to do it and I hope we have dozens of dream vacations.

So I don't know how long I was able to stay with you, I only know that it's over now for me. But, my love, it's not over for you. All those hard times that we managed to get through and become stronger are proof that you can do this now. You have one more hard time to come through and I know you'll come through it stronger. You've got to; for me and the kids, you've got to go on and get through it. I'm with you, GG, I'm with you every step of the way. I know you can't see me or hold me now, but I believe if you open your heart, you'll feel my love. It's all around you, just as it's always been. I would never let you struggle on without it. Feel me, GG, I'm with you. I'll always be with you.

I need you to do something for me. I need you to love our kids and grandkids for both of us. I know just how strong you really are, and I need you to do that. Do it for me and do it for them. I love you, GG, just as much today as the day I first knew I'd fallen for you. In fact, that love grew every single day, so I honestly love you more today.

Know that I'm watching you and loving you and that someday I'll welcome you into my arms again, but your time is not yet.

Always, always yours,

Leo

GG sat with quiet tears rolling down her face and she felt the warmth around her and the peace it brought with it. She knew that it was true, he was watching her and loving her. She also knew without the letter, she didn't know if she would have had the strength to go through this but when he asked her to love the kids for them both, there was no way she could possibly turn down that request. Leo asking it after his death had just turned it into a sacred trust for her. It was the last request he was ever going to be able to make and she had to give him what he asked for. It would be the hardest thing she ever did, but she would do it.

Chapter 15

Shelby's tears flowed as her grandmother told the story of losing Leo. Her memories of it were not very clear, faded by time and heartache. "Oh, Gran, it must have been so awful, to have him gone so suddenly."

GG smiled quietly. "It was the hardest thing I ever went through. But I knew that he was watching and I honestly could feel his love around me. And the commitment I made to doing what he asked of me kept me going when I didn't think I could."

"You have so much courage. You know, I've always seen you as the soul of the family and I'll bet Grandpa did too."

"I had forty-one years of happily married life with him. There are lots of people who never get that. I had to learn to be thankful for all I'd been given and to recognize the blessings I'd received. Leo and I had something so special and I wouldn't trade it for anything. Would you like to take a break?"

Shelby stretched and said, "Just a little one. We're getting near the end of the story, aren't we?"

GG grinned. "Soon we'll reach the present time when you know what's been happening. Starting with the new beginning,

I like to think of it, when Carter came to town to protect his feeble, old granny."

Shelby laughed. "You're not old and feeble, Gran! And I'll bet Carter found that out in a hurry, didn't he?"

"He did need to come down a peg or two. After all, what was he thinking of, investigating the girl who turned out to be his bride?"

They had their break, got themselves cold drinks and went back to finish the story.

The months that followed were a test of GG's strength and courage. Some days just didn't work, she would slip into grief and have to give herself time. But each time, she clawed her way back and refused to give up. She reread Leo's letter so many times that she had it memorized. Now she was glad that she'd always taken so many pictures that Leo would laugh at her. Now every picture was precious. The kids continued to grow up and, as kids do, they became ever more involved in their own activities and friends and, of course, for Savannah, boys. Carter was popular with the girls too, while Shelby was not quite so outgoing. But they all had a special place in their hearts for their Gran and she loved them fiercely, for herself and Leo. Missing him never stopped, the pain never went away, but she had promised to go on and she did. Somehow the months turned into years and GG learned to live with it.

Friends would try to get her to travel with them, but she was content with the traveling she'd done with her beloved Leo. Now she loved being at home in Boone, the tiny town with its residents who knew each other and watched out for each other. After more years had rolled by, she tried dating a little, but she knew quickly that Leo was the only one she would ever love or want to be with. She was content with her home and her friends and the family who never came around enough but stayed in close touch. She kept up the shop and enjoyed the work and she saw Carter graduate from college and sweep his way through corporate America, becoming a star at reviving failing corporations. Shelby graduated from college to be a first-grade teacher and she truly loved what she did. Savannah remained restless, marrying young, a much older and sinfully wealthy man whom she divorced less than a year later. He settled an enormous amount of money on her and she led the life of a jetsetter, living mostly in hotels, traveling wherever she chose, and staying with her wealthy friends when the mood struck her. All in all, they were doing well. GG just wished with all her heart that they would spend more time in Boone.

GG also had an ache in her heart when she saw her grandchildren leading single lives. She wished nothing more for them than to find the loves of their lives and the fulfillment and joy she'd had for so many years with their grandfather. She longed for the days when her grandchildren would start settling down with families of their own. The day that Maggie Maxwell came to town was the day that began the settling of her grandchildren. But, of course, that's another story.

When GG stopped talking, she smiled at Shelby and then sat up, concern crossing her face. "Shelby! Are you feeling all right?"

"I've been having this backache all day, but it suddenly seems different. I think maybe… oh! That's not just a backache!" Shelby gave a little gasp as the pain struck her and GG took a quick glance at her watch.

Twenty minutes later, GG said, "That's three contractions in twenty minutes. I think we'd better make some phone calls."

A luminous smile lit Shelby's face. "This baby's finally coming! I'll call, oops, Gran, could you call Sam?"

There was a bustle of phone calls back and forth and Sam

arrived in record time to be with his wife. He kissed her and asked, "Shel, are you all right? What can I do? I brought the bag you had packed, what do we do next?"

Shelby laughed and said, "Relax, honey, you're as nervous as a wet cat. We're supposed to head on over to the hospital."

Her husband went white as a sheet. "Oh my God, it's really happening."

GG laughed and scolded, "Now, Sam, pull yourself together. Are you okay to drive?"

He had the nerve to look offended. "Of course, I can drive."

"Okay, you get Shelby over to the hospital and I'll call your dad and we'll all meet you at the hospital. Don't worry about us, you just take care of your wife."

"Okay."

They made their way out the door and into Sam's pickup truck while GG waved from the doorway. Within a half hour, there was a small crowd at the hospital. Frank, Sam's dad, had picked GG up. Carter and his wife, Maggie, were there too, and Katie rushed in a little later, followed by Savannah and her husband, Ben. There were hugs all around and Frank and GG settled down beside each other to talk about being a grandfather and a great-grandmother. Of course, first babies usually take their time, and they had plenty of time to calm down and relax. Sam came out now and then to give them updates and finally, several hours after they had all gotten to the hospital, they took Shelby into the delivery room.

What seemed an eternity later, the doctor came out, dressed in his scrubs. "It's a baby!" he announced. "A healthy baby boy, seven pounds and four ounces, and he has a great set of lungs."

There was a babble of excited voices and more hugging.

The doctor motioned for calm. "They'll be busy for a little while and then the baby will be in the nursery while we take care of Shelby and get her comfortable. The nurse will tell you when you can get your first glimpse of the baby down at the nursery, and a little later you can see Shelby for just a little bit."

GG was teary. "Thank you, Doctor! Thank you so much."

And sure enough, a little later they were standing and looking through the glass at the beautiful baby boy Shelby and Sam had created. And finally, Maggie, who looked as if she were about to burst with good news, faced GG and Savannah and said, "Now that Shelby's had her baby, I can tell you. I didn't want to spoil her thunder, but I have news. Carter and I are having a baby too!"

The happy, noisy reaction was truly superb. GG broke down in tears and wrapped her arms around Maggie and Savannah, both together.

"Finally. Finally," GG choked out.

Carter gave her a hug. "Finally what, Gran?"

"Finally GG stands for Great Grandma."

It took the group of family and friends a while to calm down and when they did, GG was still standing at the window, gazing at the new baby. Sam joined her at the window and put his arm around her.

"Would you like to go see Shelby?" he asked.

"Oh, I sure would!"

When they walked into Shelby's room, they were followed by a nurse bringing the baby. GG carefully hugged her granddaughter and then hovered as the nurse laid the baby in his mother's arms. She sat on the bed next to them, and then Sam took a turn holding his son, and after a few minutes he turned to GG.

"GG, would you like to hold him? We have something we want to tell you."

GG held the baby as if she held the most priceless bundle in the world, which indeed he was.

"Gran, Sam and I have been talking about it for a while," Shelby said.

GG looked up and asked, "Talking about what?"

Sam said, "With your permission, we'd like to name the baby Leo."

GG caught her breath and fought back tears. "That's the most wonderful thing I've ever heard. And did anyone tell you about Maggie?"

"No, what?" Shelby asked.

"Maggie and Carter are next! They didn't want to say anything until after this gorgeous boy arrived."

"Oh, Gran, I'm so happy for them." Shelby was beaming.

GG sat there, cuddling the baby and soaking up the happiness. "Oh, Leo, look," she said softly. "We have great-grandchildren. I love you so much."

Shelby and Sam shared a kiss and GG knew that even though she was always going to feel the pain of Leo's loss, she was also always going to feel the joy of the family they had created.

Kat Carrington

Hi! I'm Kat Carrington and I write romance; sweet, spicy romance with happy ever after endings. I'm a grandmother and I'm having the time of my life letting my imagination go and telling the kind of stories that I like to read. And it's been a wonderful bonus to find out that other people like to read them too.

I was born and raised in Indiana where I raised my kids and welcomed the most amazing people into my life, my grandchildren. Having grandchildren is my greatest blessing. I'm living now in South Carolina with my always supportive hubby.

From the time I learned to read, there was always a book in my hands. After I consumed all the fiction in my elementary school library I moved on to biographies, which I found to be endlessly fascinating. Once I retired and we moved south I discovered that I was ready for a new venture. I thought back to when I was in fifth grade and sat for hours at a time at my dad's big desk writing stories with a pencil on notebook paper. One day I opened my laptop and started a story.

That first book took nearly two years to write. I'd write for a while, then forget all about it for a while. Somewhere along the way it changed from a whim to a real story that I had to finish. And that's when Blushing Books changed my whole life. My book was accepted for publication and was released on May 29, 2019. Writing is now part of my life and I hope you all enjoy my stories and the characters I keep falling in love with.

Don't miss these exciting titles by Kat Carrington and Blushing Books!

Elite 6 Assassins
Assassin's Captive

Birch Bend
Unspeakable Bonds

Dirty Politics
Crash and Burn

A Strong Man's Hand
Maggie's Match
Shelby's Secrets
Surviving Savannah
Boone Beginnings
Loving Leo
Losing Leo

Dusty Dreams Ranch
Jessie's Dusty Dreams
A Dusty Dreams Wedding

Blushing Books

Blushing Books is the oldest eBook publisher on the web. We've been running websites that publish steamy romance and erotica since 1999, and we have been selling eBooks since 2003. We have free and promotional offerings that change weekly, so please do visit us at http://www.blushingbooks.-com/free.

Blushing Books Newsletter

Please join the Blushing Books newsletter
to receive updates & special promotional offers.
You can also join by using your mobile phone:
Just text BLUSHING to 22828.

Every month, one new sign up via text messaging will receive
a $25.00 Amazon gift card, so sign up today!

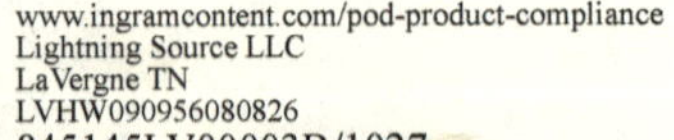
www.ingramcontent.com/pod-product-compliance
Lightning Source LLC
LaVergne TN
LVHW090956080826
845145LV00003B/1027